# Gift Horse

and other stories

Kate Cruise O'Brien

POOLBEG PRESS: DUBLIN

This collection first published 1978 by
Poolbeg Press Ltd.,
Knocksedan House,
Swords, Co. Dublin, Ireland.
© Poolbeg Press, Ltd., 1978


The generous assistance of
An Chomhairle Ealaíon (The Arts Council)
in the publication of this book
is gratefully acknowledged.


Some of these stories were first published
in *New Irish Writing (The Irish Press)*.
"Trespasses" was first published in
*Best Irish Short Stories 2,* edited by David
Marcus (Paul Elek Ltd.) and "Henry Died"
appeared in *Modern Irish Love Stories* (Pan Books).


Designed by Steven Hope
Cover photograph: Bord Fáilte

Printed by Cahill (1976) Limited,
East Wall Road, Dublin 3.

# Contents

*For Deirdre Bergson*

# Sackcloth

ASSEMBLY WAS held in the drill hall. Sarah would have preferred a high ceiling, oaken panels, and at least half a dozen former headmistresses on the walls, but at least the headmistress wore a British Legion badge and her speech was comfortingly alien.

"Christ," she said, "died for our sins." She patted her little badge which adorned a tight black décolleté bodice. Sarah wondered if that décolletage was alright. She thought not.

"It's my hope, school," Sarah raised her head; 'school' was very good indeed – "that you will play your part in the continual celebration of that sacrifice, that each of you will try to make your own small but important sacrifice to live together in unity and peace." The headmistress looked up at her green ranks – "and work to make the school thrive." Sarah allowed her eyes to fill as a hundred voices sang "To be a Pilgrim."

At four o'clock her mother collected a daughter burning with sacrifice. "Did you like it?" asked her mother, placing five gold toenails firmly on the accelerator.

"Didn't you wear shoes today?" said Sarah.

"No darling, I don't like wearing shoes to drive the car. You know that I never do."

She answered Sarah calmly. She understood very well why Sarah asked that question every time she attended a new school. Sarah had never spent more than one year at any school.

"Mother," she had said at the end of the last scholastic year, "Mother, I don't want to go back," and then cunningly, "The headmistress makes speeches about the rebirth of the Empire."

"Oh God," her mother had said. "Alright, I see your point dear, but why *will* you choose schools where they talk about Empire?"

"I'll stay next time, even if they do," said Sarah, who was leaving because her headmistress had initiated a weekly talk on "growing up". She had picked three holes in her scarlet jumper when the headmistress had talked about "our less fortunate sisters" and then walked quickly away from the pink giggling faces of her contemporaries.

"Darling," said her mother, who had decided that it was time that Sarah stopped asking the question about shoes, "darling, shoes are like the Empire."

"I know," said Sarah, looking unhappily at her mother's pale white toes.

Sarah returned with joy to school next morning. It was sunny and she could see the virtue of the drill hall. Crossbeams of dusty sun struck regularly along the rows of groomed heads. The headmistress gave a short talk about gratitude and God, sun, the continual reminder of His presence. Sarah found it disappointing. The next days and weeks it was the same. The headmistress encouraged and reassured in her assembly talks but she did not command.

At the end of assembly in the middle of term, the headmistress made an announcement. "I would like," she said, "to speak to Sarah after assembly." Sarah's classmates were not surprised. Her work, although occasionally admired and praised, was generally poor. "And she doesn't," said the pigtailed form prefect, "fit in. She never asks us to her home and it's her turn to entertain the Little Sisters of Jesus." The Little Sisters of Jesus were a Christian sewing circle, a junior mothers' union, and discussed a commandment a week. Sarah loved the Little Sisters of Jesus. Or she liked being a Sister. They lacked a leader, however, and she wished they didn't make God so vulgar. Last week He had been described as the force behind their needles, which was not, Sarah knew, a strong force.

Sarah tapped at the door. "Come in," called the headmistress. Sarah entered. "You wanted," she said, "to see me."

"Now dear, that's why, if you see what I mean," said the headmistress happily. "You are," she looked down at a page on her desk which Sarah could see was headed by her name, "obedient. You're willing to do what you are told, very willing," she smiled up at Sarah who did not smile back, "but you don't seem to understand that in this school we demand more than that. We demand active co-operation." Sarah knew that she was going to cry or to lose her temper. She could feel the muscles at the back of her knees pulling and contracting without her volition. That was a sure sign.

"But what do you want me to do," she whined and she heard the high note in her own voice as her headmistress carefully raised an eyebrow. Sarah was flattered that the other eyebrow didn't move at all.

"Dear girl," said the headmistress who was beginning to be aware that she was up against SOMETHING UNUSUAL, which was a usual enough occurrence to have been given capital letters in her mind – "We want you to join in."

"But I do try, I try so hard," and Sarah allowed herself to weep.

"Dear girl," was so delightfully, coldly, friendly.

"I do try," and then, to her lasting astonishment, she said "but my mother drives the car in barefeet," and on a high wail, "and she paints her toenails gooold." Sarah sat down and began to sob determinedly, hiccoughing and spluttering and heaving.

The headmistress, who was a kindly and intelligent woman, put her arms around her shoulders. "Does your mother like this school?" she asked.

"She doesn't care much. I mean she doesn't know what it's like. If she knew about the religion she'd say it was 'just like the Empire, darling.' I mean, really." The ugly whining voice suddenly echoed her mother's clear drawl.

"Your mother isn't religious?" asked the headmistress.

"No," said Sarah.

"Well," said the headmistress, regarding the curiously muscular hands of her pupil, "The good Samaritan." She had meant to say more but it had been quite a time since she had read that parable, and watching Sarah's right eyelid twitch she had forgotten what exactly it was that the good Samaritan did.

"She wouldn't pass by on the other side," said Sarah who was bewildered as she said this. She had just realised it herself. She wondered if her mother knew and was suddenly anxious. She saw her mother in a stupid robe helping a man out of a ditch. She began to cry again, very quietly, and was embarrassed for the first time at her own tears.

"My dear child," said the headmistress. "You mustn't let all this upset you. Your mother's heart is obviously in the right place and if she doesn't observe the forms of religion, that must be your secret little cross."

"Cross?" said Sarah, looking up.

"What you have to bear, dear," said the headmistress easily. She felt that this interview was becoming familiar once more. She regretted the intrusion of Sarah's mother, but now, it seemed, she was under control.

"I don't," said Sarah, "bear her, I love her."

"Yes, but for the sake of that love which Christ gave you, to give to your mother, you must bear her different manner of worship. All that is gold," said the headmistress, who decided that a little levity was necessary, "does not glitter."

Sarah was a singularly humourless child. "She glitters and I love her, and I love her, not Christ, and she loves me and she doesn't worship, she laughs," she added with pride, "at Bishops."

"Some of them," said the headmistress, "are quite funny."

Sarah looked at her with disgust. "They're messengers of God," she said. It was a rebuke – "and I'll have to leave. I don't think I'll be able to get used to this school."

She did not make a dignified exit. She removed herself from the chair but her stocking had caught on a nail and without pausing to disentangle it, she lifted and pulled her leg away, tearing a large hole in the stocking. She ran from the room. She knew the headmistress would ring her mother immediately, so she ran out of school without collecting her coat. This precedure didn't strike her, as it would most school girls, as lunatic or unreal. Sarah's mother accepted it and because she did that, it was natural to Sarah. She rang her mother from a phone booth.

"Mother?"

"Yes," said her mother.

"Are you wearing shoes?"

"I think so," said her mother.

"Are you wearing those pink silk slacks?" said Sarah, beginning to cry again.

"No, I'm wearing a suit."

"Will you come and pick me up now outside school," said Sarah and put down the phone.

# A Sunday Walk

IT WAS a sunny French Sunday. Elizabeth felt that life was as near perfect as it had been for a long time. At least it seemed normal. The doors of the house were open and sunlight gleamed on the black and white tiles in the hall. There were no oily barges on the river across the road, for it *was* Sunday. The river looked clear and calm and a seagull wheeled above the weeping willows which drooped at the edge of the water. She could smell a roast cooking in the kitchen. Her father was reading a newspaper in the sitting room. She looked through the door. His foot was twisting round and round in its plaid carpet slipper but she felt that carpet slippers were suitable on Sundays and surely other people's fathers twisted their feet.

Elizabeth felt it was just possible that the winter weeks of sickness and baked eggs, closed doors and tired voices had passed. She hadn't minded them really. At least while her mother lay in bed, indifferent and ill, she had found it easy to avoid school. She had said firmly that she too was ill and she had taken to her bed with an earache, a cold, a pain in her tummy. She had actually slipped on a banana skin on one of the rare occasions that she *had* gone to school. Everyone had made a great fuss because she refused to move her legs afterwards. Her mother had come, shaken and anxious, and bent over the stretcher lovingly. Like a mother in a book. However, the doctor had discovered that she could move her toes and everyone became less anxious. Still, it had been worth three weeks in bed with sympathetic adult voices reading to her in English about delightful normal children who seemed to live in a perpetual holiday world. When she'd recovered enough to go back to school she pitched · herself, somewhat ineffectively, down the stairs. She hadn't hurt her back though.

She was afraid of the school. The children there wore little aprons and spoke very fast. She didn't understand French anyway and she was always afraid that they were laughing at her. Even coming home from school was difficult. There was a long narrow tunnel leading towards their house and sometimes there was a man there in a large grey overcoat. He often pulled back the overcoat and then Elizabeth could see that he wasn't properly dressed. He'd giggle then and try to pat her head and she never knew whether she should run away fast or just smile and walk on. It seemed rude to run away. It might make the man embarrassed about not being properly dressed. She never talked to him though, because she knew she shouldn't talk to strange men. On the other hand, she never told anyone about him either because it would be difficult to talk about him not being properly dressed.

When she got home and was sitting in the warm kitchen eating greasy Irish chips cooked by the fat Wexford maid, she sometimes felt like crying because everything was so different and difficult. The cold school playground with its chilly row of latrines lining one side. The tunnel with its embarrassments. The big chilly house with its hard shiny tiles and the warm kitchen with its steamy windows. Upstairs her mother's room smelt softly powdery, the room off it where her father sometimes slept was rather dark and didn't really smell of anything. Perhaps it smelt as if no one really lived there. Her mother's room had a balcony off it. It was a bright room when the curtains were drawn back but often during the winter her mother had lain in bed in the dark. The balcony had vines growing around the little pillars at the edge. Last September before the winter came, Elizabeth had found bunches of grapes. When she picked a little bunch she found that the grapes were hard and dry and bitter as if they'd died before they were ripe. She'd often thought about the fuchsia at home. It was purple and red and if you broke off the rounded bit near the stem, sweet sticky stuff oozed out and you could lick that.

Still, perhaps the grapes would ripen this year, and in the meantime it was sunny and Sunday and there was a big sandpit in the garden where she could play all morning. It had been too cold all winter to play there. She walked out through the front door into the sun and walked towards the sandpit. As she passed the sitting room window her father called her.

"Elizabeth, would you like to go for a walk?"

"Yes. Well, where to?"

"To the piscine. You could have an orange there or an ice cream."

Last summer they'd gone to the piscine. Elizabeth had tried to swim there but the only way she could swim at all was partly submerged, which alarmed people. She looked as if she was drowning. It was nice there though, and there were tables with big umbrellas which had fringed tasselly ends. All the same, she felt like crying because her father wanted to take her there. She felt it was so kind of him but somehow rare and strange.

Her mother had departed a few days ago in a flurry of tissue paper. She'd looked well and pretty and her hair had shone with a reddish shine as if it was well again too. Elizabeth had been sorry that her mother was going away when she was well and pretty but she'd felt that if her mother had stayed, she just might have gone back to bed and felt ill again. Elizabeth admired, with a sort of breathless admiration, the kind of comforting sensible things that adults said to each other, so, when her mother told her that she'd miss her, Elizabeth said, "It will do you good to get out and have a change of air." She didn't know why air should change in different places but maybe it had something to do with different places smelling differently. Home smelt of sea and in the summer of the coconut smell of gorse in the sun. And here smelt of oil from the barges and sometimes of very fresh bread and garlic. Her mother had laughed when Elizabeth had mentioned the change of air and hugged her, but her face had looked stretched and glassy and her eyes shone as if she might cry.

And now her father wanted to go for a walk and it seemed strange to go for a walk just with her father though her father had taken her for walks during the winter when her mother was ill. She supposed it seemed strange now because her mother was away and not at home in bed.

Elizabeth felt nervous as she and her father walked along the quiet road by the river. The road was dusty and rutted and it reminded her of the lane at home which was rutted too, but muddy and lined with prickly gorse. She noticed that the spindly green bushes at the edge of this road were covered now with hanging flowers in white and purple and mauve.

"What't that flower?" she asked her father. It was an offering, for she could tell lilac when she saw it, but her father liked telling her the names of plants and trees.

"It's lilac of course," he said. "Did you never see lilac at home?"

"No, I didn't. I don't think we have it at home," she said, getting her own back for that "of course".

"Well, we do," he passed his hand over his eyes in a gesture that Elizabeth envied. It was so adult. Weary annoyance, she called it.

"I'm sorry," she said. She wished she'd stayed in the sandpit safe and warm with something to feel and touch and pour through her fingers.

"No, *I'm* sorry," said her father. "I'm just tired. Would you like to take my stick?"

The stick was beautiful. It was a blackthorn, strong and knobbly with a surprisingly smooth warm handle. Her father used to use it walking at home. He used to swing it over the ruts in the lane and thrash it through the ferns on the headland. He always walked with a straight back, his chin high in the air, and Elizabeth liked the way the stick swung out from his tall straight body.

"I'd love to take the stick, thank you."

He smiled at her as he gave her the stick and she felt like crying again. When he smiled he looked as if he'd been thinking of something else and had just remembered her, was surprised to find her there. She wished she could give him something to comfort him and as soon as she wished that, she knew that he needed comfort and she knew that she'd known this for a long time.

She'd known it on the nights that he hadn't come home before her bedtime. On those nights she'd leave an orange beside his bed in his strangely smellless room. It was something to do with her mother being away but she knew it wasn't just that. It had something to do with the fact that she'd known since her mother went away that she mustn't mention her mother to her father. Not even ask normal questions about her coming back. She'd never thought about this before. She'd just never asked about her mother and now that she had thought about it she wished her mother was here holding her, soft and safe, and she felt guilty that she wanted her mother when her father was here and sad.

# Hurt

ELIZABETH WATCHED her little boy as he wriggled around, stroking his naked chest. He loved having no clothes on. It made her uneasy, that sheer physical delight. She didn't mind it when he stroked his arms. He always stroked his sleeves when she put on his green polo neck sweater. It was synthetic but it gleamed in the light and the child would look up at the light and laugh and then he'd stroke his silky green arms and laugh again.

He was beautiful. Blond and sturdy with fine-knit tawny skin. His body was beautiful. It was strong and curved. She could understand his delight in being naked and she wondered why it made her uneasy. She was sensible and well informed. She'd read Dr. Spock. She'd even doubted Dr. Spock's well judged words. Dr. Spock doesn't approve of fathers undressing in front of their little boys. Apparently little boys sometimes play with their father's penises. Elizabeth had thought that was obvious but not very significant when she'd read it, for any child will play with a dangling toy.

Elizabeth folded up the child's plastic pants and tried to think why she should feel uneasy. It was an innocent, happy enjoyment. Perhaps it was because of that. Elizabeth didn't much like her own body. She didn't like swimming. She liked being in the water but she hated exposing her bare skin to the air. It made her feel fat. Perhaps if she'd never worried about her weight she might have liked her body a bit better.

She carefully powdered the child's bottom and put a fresh nappy on him. He liked that. She liked it too. She liked the thought of fresh new cotton wool against his dark, close-knit skin. She put away the powder and its soft, slightly spiced smell reminded her of the incense in the first church she'd ever been to.

She could remember that time very clearly because her family, in a religious country and climate, were not religious. The maid – they'd call her a housekeeper now – had taken her to Mass one Sunday. Her parents had been away. They wouldn't have objected anyway for they were very broad-minded. The church had seemed very cold. It was a sunny windy day and the walk to the church had been pleasant. It was all downhill, that walk, and great gusts of salty air had blown in Elizabeth's face. The wind had nearly blown her hat away and Mary had been cross with Elizabeth because she'd nearly lost her hat.

"Ah for God's sake child, can't you keep that hat on."

"The wind blew it off."

"You have to wear a hat in the church, you know."

"Why?"

"Because God doesn't like little girls with no hats coming into His house."

"Why?"

"Ah be quiet, because He doesn't, that's why."

The church was dusty and quiet. Mary dipped her hand in a concrete basin before she went in. Elizabeth wondered why the church had such a solid rich-looking door when the floor in the church had no carpet. The floor was made of concrete slabs like the backyard at home. It was very strange inside the church. There were seats like you had at a concert but they were harder. They were made of shiny brown wood and you could see the knots in the wood through the shine. Elizabeth knew that those dark bits were called knots because her father had had the kitchen lined with real strips of wood and Elizabeth had asked her father why he couldn't have got good wood with no dark splotches in it. Her father had laughed. "Those are knots," he said, stroking the wood the way he sometimes stroked her nose.

"What are nots?"

"Knots with a K," her father said. "They mean it's real wood."

Well maybe they did. They still looked pretty ugly to Elizabeth. They reminded her of the brown splotch on her wrist. Her birthmark. That probably meant that she'd really been born.

Elizabeth followed Mary up the paved corridor between the wooden concert seats. All the corridors seemed to lead to a table under a big window on which there were shiny vases and embroidered table cloths. There were lots of small candles in front of the table. Just before you got to the table there were railings that reminded Elizabeth of the railings at the children's playground. Mary had said that the railings at the children's playground were to stop big people from getting in. There wasn't much light in the church. All the light came through the coloured glass in the windows. The windows were pictures if you looked at them from far away. If you liked at the whole of them and not just at the different little bits.

Mary suddenly bobbed down in front of Elizabeth and Elizabeth nearly tripped. Then Mary took Elizabeth's arm and pointed at a bench. Elizabeth sat down. Mary knelt down on a plank in front of their bench. Elizabeth sat very quiet because it seemed to be that sort of place. Like the library in the village. She looked around. Nobody else seemed to be looking around. They were all bent or kneeling as if they were ashamed. There were big pictures on the wall. Elizabeth looked at the one above her. It was a picture of a man hanging from a piece of wood. She knew who that was. That was Jesus Christ, S. J. Or at least that was what her father called him. Mary never said the S.J. Elizabeth had often seen him on Mary's crucifix. The crucifix was made of brass but she'd never seen him in colour before. Mary had told her that he was nailed to the cross and left to hang there until he died but Elizabeth had never imagined that the nails had to go through his skin and bones like that and make them bleed. She'd never thought of him hanging, his body hanging from his poor torn hands like that. She felt sick. She looked for Mary but Mary was still bent before her and muttering quietly to herself. Elizabeth looked back at the picture and then she noticed that underneath his feet there was a little ledge. She hoped that it was near enough to his feet to take the weight off his poor tired torn hands.

Elizabeth sat in a sick, uncomprehending silence through Mass. Then Mary got up and bobbed again. Elizabeth was afraid to look at any more of the pictures but Mary stopped in front of one of them and said, "That's St. Veronica. I'm called Mary Veronica after her." It was another picture of Jesus Christ but he was walking in this one. His feet were safely on the ground. A woman in a long dress was holding a cloth to his face. She wore another cloth on her head, like a nun.

"Who's St. Veronica?" asked Elizabeth.

"She wiped Our Lord's face and the picture of His face came off on her handkerchief. It was a miracle," said Mary.

"Why did she wipe it?" asked Elizabeth.

"Because Our Lord was in agony," said Mary.

Elizabeth thought of those torn hands and shuddered. So that was what agony meant.

That evening Mary gave Elizabeth a bath. Elizabeth usually liked her bath. It was warm and soapy and if you were very dirty it was nice to watch the bath water run out. All the little gritty lumps running away from your soft pink body. That evening she was afraid. Her whole body seemed to hurt, but not enough. It didn't feel like her body any more. She was afraid that if she pinched herself the hurt of the pinch would be far away, like shouting and hearing your voice echo. She was afraid that if she got into the water, the hot soapy water, the heat would steam around her body and she'd feel it but her body would feel like rubber.

You couldn't say any of that to Mary so Elizabeth got into the bath. Mary went out of the bathroom to get a towel and Elizabeth sat in the bath and was afraid because she couldn't really feel the heat. She could see the steam but she couldn't feel the wet heat. She felt as if she was like a sweet wrapped up in cellophane. You could see it but you couldn't taste it.

She began to feel her own body. All the bits that usually felt most. Her nose, her ears, the back of her neck and then her breasts.

"Elizabeth," screamed Mary. "That's a sin, a mortal sin." She seized Elizabeth out of the bath. Elizabeth screamed. Mary wrapped her in a towel.

"I'm sorry little Lizzy, but you mustn't do that. Every time you do that it's another wound in our Blessed Lord's body."

"But what? Do what?"

"Touch yourself," said Mary. "You know."

Elizabeth did know. Her parents didn't much like it when she touched herself either. At least not there. But this evening she hadn't done it for pleasure. She'd done it to make herself feel real again, and all she'd done was to inflict another wound, another tear that would slide that thin body towards the ledge. But maybe he'd be more comfortable standing on the little ledge. Then Elizabeth suddenly remembered that Mary had once told her that they nailed his feet as well and she began to scream, clinging fiercely to Mary's fat creased neck.

Elizabeth picked up her baby. He was powdery and clean. His silky pullover shone against the light and she hugged him tightly against her breast, until frightened by her stiff muscles and rigid body he began to cry.

# Ashes

SARAH, WHO was inclined to be smug about her occasional stoicism, accompanied her father and stepmother to the mortuary. They were leaving flowers there for a dead friend. "I won't," she thought, watching the pebbles on the path, "be shocked. I never do cry when I should." The pebbles weren't pebbles at all, she noticed. They were cinders and they squeaked as she trod on them.

They reached the mortuary. They were just going to leave the flowers. In Sarah's family one didn't look at bodies. That smelt slightly of religion. Sarah's family didn't indulge in religion.

When she had told her father that their dear friend was going to die, she had been nervous. He might expose himself, expose an unbearable feeling which she knew she couldn't deal with. Expose the lack in their relationship. The lack of simplicity on which it was founded. Complex mutual respect, the substitute. Her father did not disappoint her. His strained innocent blue eyes watered. His hands straightened carefully on each side of his beer glass. He looked straight ahead of him into the phoney candlelight dimness of the pub. Then he looked at her. His face was pink, almost cherubic, and the water from his eyes overflowed at one corner. It was just water, though. Sarah did not feel as if it was tears.

"Did I ever tell you," he said, "about Tolstoy on his deathbed?"

"Yes," said Sarah. It was one of her father's favourite stories. "But tell it to me again." Her father was not disturbed by this disconcerting honesty.

"Well, Tolstoy" – ooy ooy echoed her mind, her father had learned Russian – "was dying and they brought priests to him. Greek Orthodox priests with tremendous long beards and flowing hair." He described them lovingly with a deliberately slow, emphatic voice – "and the priests told him: 'Count Tolstoy, you are dying, make your peace with God now,' and Tolstoy raised himself on his deathbed and said, 'Even in the presence of death, two and two still make four.'" Then Sarah's father leant back in his chair and sipped his beer. He put the glass down and wiped the corner of his eye.

When the porter suddenly drew back the sheet over the body, Sarah was shocked. It did not, that body, have anything to do with her dear friend. It was entirely dead, quite positively dead, dead as if death takes on a life of its own. Waxen, the shadows on the face browny yellow, the thin body dressed in a white robe with a blue Sacred Heart embroidered on the breast, or bust, because this body had lost a breast and gained a bust in death. The reddish hair was shorn.

Sarah remembered a graceful full figure standing in a doorway, arms outstretched, a deep voice shouting, "Ah darling, come in, come in, you are very welcome," and an enveloping comfortable embrace. A surprised embrace. She had always been surprised to see her visitors. That surprise and that loud welcome made Sarah feel that her visit was desired and desirable.

"No more shrieking," she muttered to herself as she stood by the door. There were no flowers in the mortuary, none save the sheaf they had brought. Her father stood stiffly beside her as her stepmother knelt and prayed for the departed.

"Very much departed, she's not there at all," she muttered to herself, hoping her father would hear her, convince her that two and two did still make four. Her stepmother's prayer seemed long. She kept her eyes riveted to the face. Tracing what she knew, to feel grief, to cry, to join everyone else in celebrating the departure simply. She

21

did not, however, cry, and she envied her father for knowing, perhaps, what four was. She began to hate that blue Sacred Heart. "It's disgusting,"she muttered again, another appeal, "bringing sex into it. Disembodied organs. What," she tapped her foot against the threshold, "could be more sexual?"

It was a thought craving an audience. Sarah was beginning to feel that she was unable to have any other thoughts. Her stepmother finished her prayer and they left the mortuary.

"I think she would have liked to look like that," said her stepmother who was half weeping, "so very majestic, like an embalmed saint."

"She wouldn't," thought Sarah, "have liked to be dead." She didn't say that. She didn't, couldn't be simple about this. It wasn't simple. It wasn't, any longer, a question of direct relation between herself and loss. It was unfelt pain, a stage away, just brushing her nerve ends: "like being hit on one's funny bone when one can't make up one's mind whether it's sore or a pleasure," she muttered, making the cinders squeak by hopping up and down sideways. She found that she was thinking exactly and not thinking at all. Expressing an unfelt thought, as if she were drunk.

That night she woke up at four o'clock in the morning. She was terrified. "I must," she said aloud, "stop smoking. If I start dying no one will be able to stop me. No one will care enough or understand how unbearable it is for me, because they don't want to. They'll talk about addition and majesty and that's not it at all. It isn't about final selfness, complete integrity or transfiguration. It's about the fact that I will cease to be. I won't be there, for ever." She said this aloud, but that drama didn't help. She got out of bed and looked for a sleeping pill. "Even," she said, opening a drawer. "Even in the presence." But the nothingness, the growing darkness of that image of unconscious years interrupted the chant. "Shut up!" she shouted, and hit her body but could not hurt herself. Her body was too prepared. "Oh God, let me cry. Where are those damned sleeping pills?" She found one, a something that she hoped was a sleeping pill. "If I believe it is," she crooned to herself, rocking her body, she knew obscenely, on the bed, "I'll go to sleep. Oh God, help me, help me." She began to feel drowsy and covered herself. The maid might find her half ‚undressed and half naked in the morning. One ought to be well covered in order to impart bad news, to accept sympathy, she thought, and the neatly divided years of nothingness began to fade in her mind. She tried fearfully to resurrect them. "I believe," she murmured shakily to herself, "that when I die I shall rot." It was like touching a sore tooth that had stopped vibrating with pain. It had stopped. The void did not terrify her. "The human mind," she murmured to herself or to the unseen audience that always appreciated her thoughts, "can stand only occasional moments of realisation of mortality. That's why we go on living." Rocking herself backwards and forwards in her bed, she murmured, "Oh God, help me, help me." A few moments later she felt awake again and quoted loudly:

"It is the blight man was born for,
"It is Margaret you mourn for."

That poet was a priest. Where was God then? That wasn't a question anymore. She had stopped being able to feel that for centuries, that for ever, she wouldn't know anything at all. And whispering, "God help me, help me," she went to sleep. After all, thousands of people had said it before, and in the presence of death she didn't know what four was.

# Henry Died

HENRY DIED.

University students are rarely able to cope with universals and death is the most embarrassing universal. I was shocked, and I was embarrassed.

I was sitting on the steps of the college chapel eating apples in the sun and watching people emerge from the front gate into the enclosed cobbled front square. I was counting smiles as opposed to stumbles. Some people who emerged from the dark hall, hopefully called gate, stumbed, some smiled. I was sure it was significant and was trying to make up my mind why. Then I saw my most recent boyfriend smilingly stumble out of the front gate and I picked up my newspaper. I dislike watching people approaching from a long distance or I dislike acknowledging their approach from a long distance. A greeting smile wanes somewhat after five minutes and yet one cannot cease smiling. It seems impolite. My concern over this was superfluous as he immediately crossed the square in the opposite direction. Having ascertained this, I returned to my newspaper. Then I saw Henry's picture. It was familiar to me. Peter, his best friend, had taken it the term before. There was Henry with his long pointed nose, his myopic eyes concealed by round rimless glasses and his curly hair surmounting a heading on the front page of one of Dublin's less restrained evening papers: "TCD student takes own life."

There is a rhyme:

"Mary's the one who never liked angel stories,
But Mary's the one who has died."

I always thought it was inept. It is easier to mourn the gay than it is to mourn the morose. One can write inept rhymes, one can remember their funniness with a suitable catch of the breath. The morose, who do not become life, become death even less. One should not even say that they "were somehow marked out for death." Though one does say it. The morose are usually morose through the disparity between their expectations and their reality. They are glum because life is mistreating them and they are misjudged. This however is supposed to be a comment on poor Henry who had taken his own life and it could be said that Henry had been marked out for death. He had, after all, marked death out for himself. He must have contemplated it. He achieved it, I read, with gas and sleeping pills. He had sealed up his windows and door with "Fixit — the self-adhesive that really sticks", locked the door, taken six sleeping pills and turned on the gas. "He died holding a letter from his fiancée, Miss Jennifer Carter, terminating their engagement."

Miss Jennifer Carter at that moment jumped across into the sun from the dark hallway of Front Gate. She yelled at me across the busy quiet square, "Sarah, you bitch, I've been searching for you everywhere." I smiled and waved as she bounced across the intervening space. I was never embarrassed by Jennifer's approach. We always smiled and waved and shouted in ironic acknowledgement of the difficulty of that situation, and of our enjoyment of our exhibitionism.

She reached me and grasped my shoulder. She was giggling and breathless. "I'm pissed, don't be cross, Sarah, it's such fun." She always apologised for what she hoped I would be shocked by. She liked to regard me as her strict mentor from time to time. It added interest to two mild glasses of shandy.

I handed her the paper. She read the column, handed the paper back to me and sat down beside me. She picked up an apple and began to eat it in large bites, munching and swallowing it quickly.

"I've known that, Sarah. They rang Henry's parents rang last night and told me."

"Well why didn't you tell me?"

She fiddled with a corner of her eyelash (false) and looked across the square.

"Because I didn't know what to say. I don't know how to deal with this."

"You don't have to say anything, not to me, anyway, but when you do, don't pretend it was your fault or that you have to feel guilty. All right, you're sorry. You were engaged to him. You once thought you were in love with him and you'll have to see people blaming you because you discovered you weren't. You might make that easier for yourself if you rushed around saying it was your fault and that you felt guilty. People would pity you. It would be bad for you, though, and untrue. You might get to believe it, and no one, no one is responsible for taking their own lives but themselves. Don't dramatise it, Jenny, it's a supreme situation for self-dramatisation and you mustn't do it because this time self-dramatisation is dangerous."

She had watched me carefully throughout this speech. "You're dramatising, you're acting the wise friend, the knowing confidante. And I don't know why you're so defensive about my guilt." And then she grasped my wrist and began to laugh, hiccupping pieces of half-chewed apple out of her mouth. She coughed then and choked, and I withdrew her grasp from my wrist and thumped her back until she stopped choking. She looked at me again.

"I could have cried then, laughing to tears, but I won't, I promise. Let's go away from here." And so we went.

Despite my homily, I began to realise the next morning why Jennifer hadn't told me until she had to. I did not at all know how to deal with this situation and I was very tempted to pretend it had not happened. But I had gone out with Henry's best friend the term before and I loved Jennifer. Since I could not pretend with them, I could not pretend with anyone, for acting over something as large as this would have to be an uninterrupted business.

Jennifer, I saw, when I arrived in the coffee bar, was definitely dressed for a part, which I noted commenced with everyone else's knowledge of Henry's death, not with her own. She was wearing a very dashing black floppy hat, with a veil which half-covered her face, a brown and white checked coat, and a black dress.

I looked at her as I sat down on the bench beside her. She was smoking a cigarette with difficulty because of the veil, and also because her fingers were shaking.

"Why are you wearing that thing?" I asked, nodding at the hat.

"Isn't it gorgeous! I think I look mysterious and dangerous." She lifted the veil a little and peered out at me.

"And a little, little bit tragic?"

"No," I said.

"No, I didn't think so either, really." She opened her handbag and took out a pair of dark glasses. She then lifted the veil and put them on and lowered it again.

"More mysterious, more dangerous, Sarah?"

"Yes," I said. Then I paused. "Jennifer, what did you say to Henry's parents?"

"Oh, I was quite terse really, you know, 'yes, no, how, when?'"

"Were they nice about it?"

"Well," she said, or drawled with consideration. She is accurate and careful in her assessment of behaviour. "It was his mother, and she was really very nice to me. And it was a bit difficult for her because I was so terse. So she said I should come to the funeral, which is tomorrow, and then she said something at the end like 'You mustn't blame yourself, my dear, and you must let your feelings go, have a good cry.' The main idea was that underneath my tough exterior there [8]s a heart of pure molten gold, that I was pretending not to care when I did really."

"Do you?"

"I don't care," she said. "I didn't depend on him any

more, and if someone is dead, and one doesn't see them dying, and one didn't depend on them, how can one care?"

She took off her glasses and I saw that the skin around her eyes was puckered and red. Above her eyes she wore her usual rather strange make-up. Wispy black lines were drawn out in a radius from a black socket line. From her eyes to her eyebrows her skin was painted a light blue-white. The veins of her eyelids showed through the paint.

"Have you been crying?"

"A bit, but it's more or less acting to myself really, and worry because I'm frightened of meeting people."

"You mustn't, love. The people who matter will know you well enough not to blame you."

"Do you really think they shouldn't blame me?" It was a question I didn't want to answer.

"Are you coming to this lecture?" I asked. She pulled her long hair. Her hair was inclined to be very wavy and grew unevenly. It was one of her permanent and irregular attractions, for it stood out around her head like a jagged brown and yellow cloud in blurring bars of colour. Jennifer put a yellow end of hair in her mouth and sucked it. "No," she said, out of the other side of her mouth.

"Will you be all right?" We allowed ourselves to look after each other, for although we were aware of the occasional excess of our concern, or because of our awareness of it, we were never embarrassed by our own sentimentality. It was like talking to oneself to cheer oneself up.

"Yes, love," she put a hand on my shoulder. "Run along, Sarah, and I'll be a big brave girl, big certainly." She giggled. She was tall with very big bones, but not fat. Her figure was a constant source of worry to her and again, as in the case of her hair, in not conforming to the skeleton standard of conventional beauty, it held an attraction of its own.

I went out of the coffee bar and walked along a line of low Elizabethan rubrics towards my lecture, which was in an ugly, but not obtrusive building in the square behind. As I turned the corner I saw Peter coming towards me. Peter and I together had formed, for a short while, a foil for Henry and Jennifer. Or, as Jennifer said, "I got you and Peter together, love, to mitigate the boredom, the ghastly, intolerable boredom."

"Sarah, I want to talk to you," said Peter.

"Yes, I'm going to a lecture, but I don't have to go. I think we should talk. I mean —" I stumbled on the cobbles and, as Peter put out a hand to help me, I bent my head. I am incapable of exchanging looks with men I care for.

"Come for a walk," said Peter. "Around College Park." We walked into College Park, where young men in track suits were training by running slowly around the periphery of the shorn grass. We both sat down on a bench and, for a time, sat still. Peter watched the runners and I watched the trees which grew around the sides of the park. They were large elms. The sun shone through them, dappling the long grass at the side of the track. I could see two friends of mine lying side by side, their heads against the bole of a tree. The man was tickling the girl's neck with a twig.

"How does Jenny feel now?" asked Peter. He turned his head towards me. I thought that I had forgotten how big his nose was and his chin.

"How do you mean 'How does she feel'?" The young man had abandoned his twig and now gently eased his arm under the girl's neck.

"About Henry." The girl settled her head against the man's shoulder and I could see her two white feet twisting.

"Sorry, but not guilty. She shouldn't, you know, feel guilty. Henry never tried to help himself whenever she broke it off. He just ran around after her and asked for more."

"You are a bitch, Sarah. I mean that." Peter bent over towards me. His eyes, which were big and blue, opened widely. The muscles at one side of his nose contracted and the corresponding side of his mouth lifted. He achieved a

29

sneer. He had large features, big eyes, a large crooked nose and a long chin. His cheeks were fleshless. Until I met Peter I never believed that there was such a thing as a gaunt face. His was gaunt. When he smiled his face did not relax, it tautened, and the skin around his eyes wrinkled. His whole face was used in his smile, and when he sneered now I felt a little sick.

"I liked Henry, he did Jenny good, he made her grow up a lot." I lied, and then was afraid that Peter knew that I was lying and would despise me for betraying the integrity of my own feelings, and then I thought that I was not betraying my integrity, for my first feeling was of wanting Peter. I knew that was a lie, for if I had to change myself to please Peter, wanting Peter was an illusion, but I knew I wanted Peter. These thoughts made themselves felt in an unhappy confusion which resolved itself in uneasiness and a sudden desire to cry and run away, to go home and wait until Henry had been forgotten.

"Yes, Henry did help Jenny, and he really loved her. She just used him. She kept the engagement going until Trinity Ball because she wanted a partner, and she kept herself amused in the meanwhile by having constant rows with him. I went through it, Sarah. I sat up with him each night after their constant quarrels. And I know what he felt like because I've been through that too." As he spoke, he lowered his voice. I suppose he thought that I would be moved. But I was too much at his emotional mercy to pity him now for his past and vague sufferings. Also because I felt *I* was to be pitied I was sure *his* self-pity was insincere. I did not, of course, say this to him. Because I act so constantly I hate catching other people out in their little acts.

"You don't know what Jennifer felt like."

"Why don't you tell me?"

"She acts, you know. The quarrels weren't real to her, they just alleviated the boredom."

"Boredom?" asked Peter. His face seemed to fall away from his eyes now and he swept his hair back from his face dramatically, but ineffectually.

"Is that all it meant to her?"

"No, it isn't at all all it meant to her. It was just extra."

"Extra?" He was really quite funny with his one-word interjections. Peter truly has an expression that represents to me all the things that I associate with the word quizzical. He can look attractive, questioning and amused all at the same time. I feel then like a young and intelligent child who has been so clever that her schoolmaster almost loves her. The expression was there now and, in response, I was clever.

"She loved his love, you see. It was the one thing in Henry she felt above all others, and by quarrelling she could see it working."

"There were, eh" – the "eh" sounded silly – "other ways of seeing love work?" I was disappointed in him and I deteriorated. Back to amateur Freud, the bane of my young life, when I couldn't be ill without my clever elder sister telling me that it was only my unconscious.

"She didn't trust those ways." I felt uncomfortable. I couldn't say sex. Not to somebody I'd been to bed with.

"She felt that those ways were the only reason Henry wanted her, and she kept on having to remind him they weren't."

"That's nonsense."

"I know," I said, and was pleased that Peter should think it was nonsense. I like people knowing I'm being trite when I am being trite.

"Well, if you know, don't try and justify her. She just wanted to manipulate Henry, and she did, out of existence. A great power game." I felt very shaky. Peter said the last sentence with a pause after each word and I felt a terrible impulse to giggle, and once I started to giggle I knew that I would be unable to stop. I decided to pretend to cry instead and curiously, once I let the hiccupping motion which was in my stomach out, I was crying.

"Don't do that, Sarah." He patted my shoulder from behind. Not caressingly. Just trying to stop me. "Don't get

31

yourself torn up by this, don't make yourself believe that Jennifer was justified and then get upset because you can't convince yourself, and you can't feel sorry for Jennifer and Harry at once." Peter saying Harry made me cry again. Because of the late-night coffee sessions they had together, their camaraderie, their being funny together. At last I did feel sorry and, more than that, unhappy, that Henry was dead.

"Don't, Sarah, I can't leave you like this. Here." He gave me a large, dirty handkerchief and I mopped my face with it. I refrained from blowing my nose, though I wanted to. "Look, if you face the fact that your defence is useless to Jenny and you, you'll be a lot better off. The most important thing now is that Henry is dead and he died because Jennifer was too occupied with her frivolities to see that his feelings for her were entirely serious. That must have been terrible. Feeling so much and never getting a response that wasn't calculated, for effect."

I blew my nose. I decided that it was, after all, childlike and endearing to blow the nose. "I know that, Peter."

"Well, don't defend her then."

"It is nothing to do with defending her. Jennifer acts. That's Jennifer. It was a terrible accident."

"All right, she acts, but she should have gone somewhere else to act. She should have seen that Henry wasn't acting. It was not seeing that's unforgivable, and if she refuses to see her guilt that's even more unforgivable." I was pulling a button on my coat, and as I tightened my hand the thread broke and it fell to the ground. Peter picked it up and gave it to me.

"Didn't you see that, Sarah?"

"Yes, I suppose I did." I had, of course. It is easier not to realise something one does not want to realise alone. When someone one respects realises it for one it is unhappily inescapable. Now I had been forced to face her guilt, which was considerable, and appalling to me because she did not seem to have recognised it at all. I had tried to avoid thinking about her guilt because I did not want to be separate from her. To disapprove of her without her approval.

We got up to go by common, but mute consent. We had nothing else to say to each other and I needed to see Jennifer.

As we approached the coffee bar I saw Jennifer peering out of the window. Her hat had slipped back on her head and the veil of the hat was now covering, not her eyes, but her hair. I did not tell Peter I could see her, although I knew he had seen her and though I knew he knew I had seen her.

"Thank you for the walk," I said. I wouldn't have said that if I could have thought of anything else to say, or if I could have borne silence. Silence was embarrassing between us now. We were neither companionable nor uninterested.

"What are you thanking me for?" asked Peter.

"For nothing, obviously, if you can ask that."

"How do you mean 'if you can ask that'?" Now that Henry was dead, the only subject on which we could talk with any ease at all was his death. Every other subject would be affected by that fact. Because any other subject would be an escape from the embarrasment of Henry's death, which was much less embarrassing than the escape. At least that was what I felt Peter felt. What I knew was that the escape was from the sudden absence of intimacy between us, which left us with no knowledge of how to deal with each other. I felt regret for this, but I wanted the ending to be over.

Jennifer came out of the coffee bar. Her veil was back over her eyes.

"I must go, Sarah. I'll see you sometime." The sometime meant he wouldn't see me. The he looked at Jennifer as she came up and smiled, or grinned. For the smile was concentrated towards one end of his mouth and his nose wrinkled.

"What a hat, Jennifer, are you by any chance Miss Garbo wanting to be alone?"

33

"I vant to be alowne," said Jennifer.

Peter laughed, waved and left us. I both admired and despised him for his manner with Jennifer. I admired him because I hate scenes and I dislike coolness, and I despised him because he ought to have addressed his complaints about Jennifer to Jennifer. I knew that in the same situation I would have behaved in the same way. Unfortunately for me, I always hope that my men will have greater integrity than I have myself. Integrity is a quality that I admire because I find it so hard to possess it. I would rather be liked than to sit in judgement because I would rather be protected than be the protector.

"Let's go to the park," said Jennifer. She grabbed my arm and I clung to it.

"Thank God for you, Jenny."

She lowered her glasses and looked at me. "Was it that bad?"

"Worse."

"Is it over?"

"I can't think of any way it wouldn't be."

The park was empty now. The lovers had gone and whitish clouds had come over the sun. They were low clouds, for one of them raked the top of the trees and began to look like mist, fading from cloud to thick air to air.

"What did Peter say?"

"Nothing much."

"Did he say anything about me?" A small piece of cloudy mist seemed to be caught in a branch of the tree. The two ends of it moved slowly apart and together, embracing the branch and then letting it go.

"I'm not going to the funeral."

"Why not?"

"Because there'll be all those people knowing it was my fault."

"Knowing?"

"You know it was, don't you, Sarah? I've been thinking about it. I know it was my fault because I've enough knowledge of psychology to know that that's why I'm afraid of people thinking it was. But I don't know it for any other reason. I mean I don't feel guilty."

I was released from blaming Jennifer because as soon as she knew it was her fault, I didn't have to know for her. It was a shared, not a separating motion. But I still didn't see what the trouble was.

She sat on the grass, which was moist, for the mist was gradually thickening and dampening. She dug little holes in the grass with her bare fingers. "Sarah," she said, and her voice was very high, "I don't feel anything at all. I know everything and I don't feel anything, and I know everything because I've been informed. I do really want to feel something."

And a line came into my head:

"Oh God, I believe. Help Thou my unbelief."

# A Gift Horse

I WAS prepared for the evening; I had made a list:
1—Bath.
2—Manicure.
3—Wash hair.
4—Clean flat, not just tidy, but clean it.
5—Wash clothes.
6—Get early night.
As if I needed an early night, or cared if I should need it. But it looked very nice at the end of the list. "Get an early night." It was such an anxious, affectionate command to myself. Then the bell rang. At least the bell went ding-dong. I lived in a "modern" bedsitter which was "modern" because it had a tiny hall, in which I delighted, and it boasted a bell that went ding-dong.

"Please let it be no one I'm seeing later in the week."

I hate people to upset my plans, my map of the week. This evening was empty but I had planned it out of emptiness. I had anticipated it. I could not bear that one of my engaged evenings later in the week should be taken from me because I knew that it would remain irredeemably empty, a failed social evening, not a holiday with myself. I went to the door and opened it. There was a man standing on the shallow doorstep. Modern bedsitters also have shallow doorsteps. It makes them seem like separate dwellings.

"Yes," I said. I did not recognise him.

"Sarah, you look just the same."

"Do I?" I said cruelly. I was still certain that the joy of an unexpected call must anger my fates and that I was about to pay for it.

"The same as what?"

"The same as you did seven years ago, when you said that we should see each other in seven years."

"Did you rehearse that?" I asked, still leaning against the door frame. I was delighted with the romantic tenor of the conversation. Such things always happen to beautiful ladies in books, but never to me. I felt suddenly capable of the sparkling yet unexcited dialogue that these ladies inevitably managed to maintain.

"Yes," he said, which upset me. It didn't fit into the dialogue.

"Well, come in." And I felt now completely at a disadvantage and guilty because I could not remember who he was.

"Do come in."

"I'm Stanley, you know."

"My God, you've changed then," I shouted. I should have remembered him. Stanley had balanced precariously on a wire thread between endearing pomposity and affectedness. He had usually managed to be precisely pompous.

"Come in, come in." I tugged at his sleeve. I was no longer at a disadvantage. I had always been in charge where Stanley was concerned. He came in and was impressed by my little hall.

"Let me take your coat," I said graciously, and as he took it off I took it from him and hung it up on a coathook.

"Come and have a drink."

"But you said then that I could take you out to dinner and we'd discuss how you'd improved and I'd deteriorated." Stanley's large wide nose contracted with displeasure.

"Well, I must have been an arrogant little bitch," I said, busily disassociating myself from that outspoken reflection of myself. "And I have improved. I wouldn't say that *now*. Have a drink anyway and we'll see about dinner afterwards." I inspected the three bottles on my desk. There was, as I expected, a very little cider in the end of each one. I never quite finish my bottles of cider. I believe that not finishing them represents economy and look forward to the day when I will pour all the ends into one splendid large bottle and have it, as it were, for free. I picked out two of the least grubby glasses and poured the cider ends into them.

"To those seven years," said Stanley gallantly, waving his glass around. I put my glass down on the table beside me without drinking the toast. I thought it might be unlucky to drink to those seven years. They might repeat themselves or something.

"What," I said "is your emotional condition, Stanley?" I remembered that I had always been able to ask him pertinent questions with ease. I used to be in love with myself when I went out with Stanley. He wanted to be examined because he was too lazy to examine himself so he presented himself, with faith, to my scrutiny. I can still see him sitting in the coffee bar. The light had caught his shiny nose and he was saying, "Yes, you're right, you're wise Sarah," as I berated him for cowardice and purposelessness. I was envious of that memory of myself which he had evoked. I used to be so certain.

"I am married," he said. "She's not very clever but she does something for me. She needs me to make decisions for her and when I do make them she is beautiful with amazed admiration. Then," he looked at me and smiled, "the decisions have to work, don't they?"

"I suppose so," I said. "I used to sit and wait for your decisions to fail dismally in their effect, that's what you mean, isn't it?"

Stanley, having made his point, could afford to be generous. He came over to my chair and stood in front of me. He was short and slightly bowlegged. He put out one hand and placed it on my shoulder.

"What I used to like about you was that you were brave. You used to commit yourself wholly and you never left yourself any insurance against getting hurt." His large, pink-encircled eyes looked purple as they became round with irritated anxiety. "I did hurt you, didn't I?"

I was astonished. He was either behaving out of character or he had changed into confident arrogance. I felt foolish because I had been talking to a familiar Stanley, patronising the man I knew seven years ago. I was annoyed with myself and therefore I resented him.

"No," I said. "You ran away before *I* could hurt *you*." It was crude but I was angry.

"Ah, I see," he said, returning to his chair. "That, of course," (he emphasised the "of course"; I suppose he thought he was being ironical) "was how it was."

"Stanley," I said, "why did you come here if you wanted to abuse me? Whatever I did or said seven years ago is irrelevant. You really cannot pay me back now."

"I'm not paying you back," he said. "I came to see how you were. That's not very good, is it? Grubby, sordid and empty." He looked at his glass and I was embarrassed because it did not shine in the light. "I wanted to find out about your . . ." he paused to indicate that the phrase was not his . . . "emotional condition."

"Stanley, dear Stanley," I said, relenting for the sake of beautiful dependence. "You are a pleasure to me. There is nothing I would rather describe." And I described it in detail.

I sat on my desk three hours later inspecting a new cider bottle. There was an inch left so I put a stopper on the bottle and opened another new one.

"I still don't really believe that there's no hope," I said, looking at him though he had listened with attention and response for the last three hours. "You know, I still say to myself that something I will say or do the next time I see him will make him realise how indispensable I am. I spend hours thinking out ways of making myself indispensable but he's never there for long enough." Stanley laughed and I saw that the crease lines around his eyes were now quite deep.

"Then you'll never be indispensable except as a once a week joy, will you, Sarah?"

"No," I said. "But it seems silly to give that up while I can still have it."

"Except," said Stanley, running his finger around the rim of his glass, "that you want to get married and he, apparently, is not on the market."

I got a sponge from the sink beside me and wiped the counter around me. The neatness was an effort against my natural condition of squalor.

"I don't know that he's not. That's what I'm afraid of — that I'll go away after all this time when, if I stayed, I might marry him."

"Well, go away, and if he needs you, if there was ever any possibility of marriage, it will occur to him then." It was very simple of course. I knew that he was right and that he understood my dilemma. Understood that the terror of missing something, the if onlys of after I went away, were what had kept me. His percipience annoyed me. He had no right to understand. I was the one who had inspired him to accurate action seven years ago.

"You *do* know," said Stanley, rubbing one finger gently up and down his thigh. "You don't seem to have the strength for action though."

It was that statement which decided me. I wanted to resurrect the assurance that he had seen in me. I was envious of what I had been.

"I will," I thought, as I got out of bed the next morning, "break it off." At six o'clock I was ready to go out and Phillip was late. The flat was, for once, clean. I had cleaned it as a kind of preparation for a new way of life. I looked around at the shining, polished furniture and thought that it would be a pity if Phillip did not come, if he was not there to see how well I could get along without him. Besides, I thought, after seven years I deserve a farewell scene. And it was my birthday.

The door opened and Phillip threw down three bunches

of flowers on the floor and lifted me in the air.

"Put me down, you ridiculous man," I screamed. I was afraid that he was going to prevent me from being tragic. "I mean it," I added crossly. I was annoyed. He held me above his head and I looked at his black and white-streaked hair. It was short and curly. "It *would* streak," I thought, in an effort to think viciously. "He couldn't just go grey like anyone else."

"The birthday girl, the lovely twenty-eight year old lady. We present her to the world." Then he let me slide down his body and held me in his arms.

"Happy birthday," he said in a low voice. I knew he expected me to be moved. And I *was* moved and sorry for him because he did not know that he had no longer any right to expect it. He kissed the top of my head. "And here is your birthday present." He took from his pocket a silver bracelet and held it out.

"I don't want it," I said, retreating backwards.

"You don't want it." He frowned. "My God, you don't want it," he shouted. He flung the bracelet across the room and then he picked up the three bunches of flowers and tried to tear them in pieces. The paper tore but the flower stalks only bent. Flowers bound and wrapped in tissue paper will not tear cleanly. His face went red and his strong hands whitened, but the thin stalks, forced together in his hands, would only bend.

"If you broke them one by one, or took off their heads or something," I said kindly, "it would look very nice." He looked at me. There was some white spittle on his chin from his roaring. His coat was still on and it was damp. He looked ridiculous, in angry, suspended motion.

"I didn't mean it," I said. I could not bear that he should look ridiculous. "I do want the bracelet."

After he had left I arranged the flowers as an offering to Stanley.

# The Glass Wall

THE PUSH chair broke. It was as simple as that. The vomiting world decided not to get sick after all. And I grabbed the baby, righted the push chair and took my son home. Before I reached home I had stopped shaking and the symptoms of panic – they call it agoraphobia, fear of open spaces – had ceased.

It was, and possibly always will be *my* agoraphobia. I don't use that "my" with pride. No, not like "my period". Ah yes, what an achievement, what a little woman and, finally, there's another to suffer. No. It's not like that. There is no community of abnormal suffering, and what does such suffering produce except fear. *My* agoraphobia is a source of shame, a crippling thing, even a disgusting thing. I shake, I tremble and I'm afraid of my Judgement. The judgement for smoking forty cigarettes a day and drinking an amount that I can never remember is eternal death, or fear of it, which is worse. Fear of darkness and the unknown.

With one dear small fat hand clinging to mine I decided to defer fear of that darkness till later and hang on.

The fear had been riding me, clinging to me, my old man of the sea, for years. Two, to be precise.

It started in Sheffield. I had gone shopping with a friend. I was attempting to buy two pairs of black pants (large) in Marks and Spencers when it happened. Well it didn't *happen*. I did it to myself. Much comfort. I was walking across a large shiny tiled floor, which believe it or not was warm. It looked cold. It should have been cold but my foot left damp steaming imprints on the cool white glaze. Then the flickering lights started to bother my eyes. I mean my eyes felt as if someone had fired a handful of salt into them. I didn't connect the stinging in my eyes with the flickering of the lights. My body was a jammed switchboard, each signal registering ALARM. Out of my control. I knew with no doubt whatsoever that I was going to die then. Right there on Marks and Spencers' shining hot plastic floor. Fall down dead in front of innumerable embarrassed shop assistants (all clad in plastic and possibly hot).

I looked for my friend frantically but my eyes wouldn't focus. I was afraid to look at any one point for very long. I was afraid that heaps of cheap underwear might dissolve and melt as my senses failed me, as I died. God knows I'd read enough accounts of the signs of death. Blindness, deafness, all at the last minute. I might hoodwink death by not looking or hearing, by not trying to anyway since death might see to it that I couldn't.

I ran towards the nearest person who might hold out a hand and stop me from dying. I felt that ladies in plastic coats could help. It wasn't the white plastic hospital coat I sought. It was just, at that time, that dying seemed abnormal and ladies in plastic coats, beautifully normal. I felt that such ladies couldn't be witnesses to anything as terrible as my death. Well, I was wrong. They took my fear calmly, those ladies. As soon as they saw me they recognised me. On the other side. Sick, ill, imagined or otherwise, we don't want to know. They brought me water as I sat on a hot plastic seat. I gulped and gulped. One of them said "Don't drink it so fast. It's two flights up."

"What is?"

"The tap."

Well they were probably right. The tap, the wear and the tear, the baby that cries in the night, the one person you have to be nice to because you couldn't bear to be uncharitable. Those demands, accepted, add up to a person who can't, won't and is too embarrassed to ask for any help. Except by making themselves so sick that sheer fear of that sickness will drive them beyond the limits of ordinary good manners. I rushed beyond those limits. It was as if I'd been awaiting my moment to knock down a few barriers here and there for years.

Marks and Spencers' white plastic ladies had alerted my friend. The water had failed. I just kept drinking it. So Marks and Spencers alerted the wine of friendship.

"Anne," I said, as she held my water glass, willingly relinquished by the white plastic brigade. "I'm having a heart attack."

She knew I wasn't. She told me to relax, to lie down, come home, have tea. In the end she took me in a taxi (I wanted an ambulance) to hospital.

The doctor in the out-patients department recognised me instantly. He deserted the woman bitten by a dog (her hand was still throbbing and it had happened three weeks ago) and said he'd take me. I was desperate by then and indignant. I mean, I was dying wasn't I. The nurses, incredibly, had told me to take my turn.

The doctor was kind or interested. It was as if he saw me across the palpitating glass wall that had come between me and the outside world. As if he understood that die today or die in thirty years, the fear of it is the same. He examined me most patiently. He was brave because the nurse was quite cross with him and kept on telling him about the lady who was bitten by the dog.

"Yes, I know," he said. "But this is interesting."

It was good to be interesting but I wonder what I would have felt like if I hadn't been.

After a few moments of sounding and pressing and feeling he said: "Why are you nervous? What are you afraid of?"

Well if you must know, of dying, that first. After that I'm afraid of being found out. My husband's bound to find me out. I'm not anything. I've nothing to give. In fact, (with a hideous leer) there's a lot I'd like to *take*.

Well, I didn't say any of that. I said, and it was true, "Of bombs."

Then he looked at me and said in a sad voice: "Of course, you come from Ireland."

I admitted it. My hands started to shake again and the easy endless tears began. I'd found something, something that couldn't possibly be my fault or blame. Oh if they'd made thirty odd people into corpses couldn't they have crippled me in my mind.

Half Dublin claimed, with some pride, that it had missed death by inches. It wasn't difficult to make such a claim. Three evil cars in narrow streets. A bus strike and a horde of weary innocent commuters trying to make their way to the trains.

A loud bang from a place some space away. I ran towards it and I saw a man, a large man being carried by two others. The man's trousers were torn and his hairy legs were bleeding. Then I saw a car burning in high merry flames. Those flames were quite busy, just like an ordinary fire. Crackling away. I asked a woman what had happened and she said, "That car blew up."

She said it grimly, as if it had been the car's fault.

I looked around and I saw a black leather boot on the ground. Above the boot there was a thick woolly rug. The boot was new. I'd wanted a pair like that yesterday.

That was the trouble, it could have been me.

The push chair, however, did break down and I had to take that fat hand in mine and walk its dear owner home. It wasn't his fault, after all.

# Trespasses

"I JUST don't happen to fancy you when you're fat."

She had been sitting at the kitchen table when he came in. She'd felt happy that evening. The house was clean, the supper was ready and the diet had worked. The weighing-scales had registered a satisfactory eight stone that morning so she'd had an extra glass of cider before he came home. What she had perhaps forgotten was that cider tended to distend her stomach and that sitting at the kitchen table in her tightest sweater was scarcely flattering to a slight midriff bulge. She had never been able to believe that looks mattered that much, that a bulge here or there could dissolve love, distract attraction. Looks didn't matter to her. She didn't mind if he were fat or thin so long as he loved her.

To his fastidious eye her bulges, her sloppiness and her grubby face were an affront. A denial of affection. He kept on finding squashed-up dirty handkerchiefs in the drawer where she kept the knives and each time he found one of these hideous, smelling bundles he hated her because her love was so careless. He felt that having, incredibly, gained his love she could be more careful with it. She should tend it with good cooking, tidy house-keeping, made beds and apple pie. Above all she should tidy herself up. Joanna was not like that. She would cook gourmet meals every day for a week, scrub floors. She had a most peculiar and energetic attachment to the kitchen floor which she scrubbed and polished whenever she was seized by a mood of dynamism. That was the trouble, he thought. Joanna was subject to moods. She was seized by them, tossed by them, driven by them like a piece of old newspaper in a high wind. And then the wind would die down and she'd take out the six-pack of cider and sit bulging over the kitchen table as the dust on the furniture settled and the bed was left, rumpled and stained, upstairs.

"Well, don't fancy me then. Find yourself a thinner model if you want. See if I care." She stamped out of the kitchen, banging the door behind her, and he examined the contents of the pots on the stove gloomily. She'd made a rather coarse and careless spaghetti sauce that seemed to owe something to tins and little to ingenuity. Of course whatever she said now, however angry she was, his words would take effect. She'd be nervous in the morning. He could almost hear the clang of the scales in the bathroom, for years his first morning sound. Frightened of losing his love, she'd clean and scrub and cook with care. She'd rush around the house with cups of coffee and little snacks. She'd get grimy herself, of course, and that was what he resented. Why didn't she look after herself, keep herself tidy, wash her own hair instead of warming towels to dry *his* wet hair. She was a spasmodic selfless torrent like the fizz from her own cider bottles. Her indulgences were almost masochistic. Well, he thought, as he carefully sieved the lumpy spaghetti sauce, who else would diet for a week and then blow themselves up with cider.

Joanna lay in bed, crying. He'd said it. He'd said it at last. The one unforgivable thing. She'd been waiting for it. God knows she'd been waiting for it. She'd always wondered if it was possible for someone you loved and needed, above all needed, to say anything that *was* unforgivable. She had read more bad novels than most people and in those glimmering, rainbow, soapsud worlds people did say unforgivable things. People who loved each other. Now that she came to think of it, those novels rarely mentioned need. You love out of passion, not out of need. Well now he'd said it. He'd thrown her back to the nervous time where he had found her.

It was at a party at the height of her hilarity. She'd just

47

left home and she was living in a flat. She was frightened of her own daring. She knew that even on a privileged middle-class allowance she couldn't afford it. So in order to forget the overdraft she'd gone to the party. A lot of Joanna's life at the time was ordered like that. She had been flirting wildly and desperately with a rather unpleasant bearded man, who, to her alarm, suddenly responded and asked her to dinner. Frightened by this success she moved away abruptly and bumped against Timothy. She spilt his drink over her dress and he apologised, for what was, after all, her fault.

"It was my fault," she said.

"Yes," he said, and looked at her glass which was tilted dangerously over his jacket sleeve. His abruptness acted on her as inevitably as nature fills a vacuum. She had attached herself to him for the rest of the evening and he had found himself taking her home. On the way home, out of some impulse of affection for his withdrawn, freckled face, she had kissed him and he let her.

He'd let her marry him. Joanna rubbed some of the mascara off her sodden eyelids and considered that. Words resounded in her tired cider-dampened brain. Unforgivable. Let her. Allowed her. Suffered her. Suffer the little children. All right, she knew she was childish. She knew that she over-emphasised her own meticulous sense of disorder to a stage where it became grotesque. But if she hadn't been childish, hadn't needed and depended on him, she would never have had the desperate courage to marry him.

Timothy was living with her when the idea first occurred to Joanna. The idea had come naturally, as it were, because she thought she was pregnant. She went to the doctor immediately. The doctor was a fat, jovial woman. She was known as the "Pill doctor" because she was one of the few doctors in Dublin who would prescribe contraceptives. She knew Joanna.

"I hope you have a regular boyfriend this time."

"Oh yes, it's not that. I don't want the Pill."

"Oh," said the doctor, "you think you're pregnant?"

"Yes."

"What do you want to do about it then?"

As the implications of these words sank in, Joanna knew that she wanted the baby.

"Oh," she said, "I'd like it to be a girl," and because the doctor had few cheerful moments, dealing as she did with a torrent of hysterical, lovelorn girls, she smiled.

"You'll keep it, I mean if you're having it?"

"Oh yes."

Warmed by the doctor's smile, Joanna saw herself bending over a cot. She saw herself pregnant and glowing with approaching motherhood. When she got home she told Timothy that she thought she was pregnant. He looked to her. All he could see was an encroaching bulge.

"What would you do about it if you were?"

"I'd keep it."

"You could go to London."

"No, I couldn't do that. Say it had been me and I hadn't lived, I'd been destroyed."

He sighed. Joanna had a talent for talking like the books she read. He wondered what triumph of emotional blackmail she was coming up with now. How was she going to glue him to that encroaching bulge.

"I wouldn't get rid of it. I'd have to get rid of you though. I mean I couldn't marry you for a reason like that," she said, handing him back a gift that had not been offered. "You know my family," she went on (and on he sometimes thought), "they wouldn't approve of you not marrying me. You'd feel dreadful, so you'll have to leave here if I *am* pregnant."

Joanna spent a week looking forward to the baby, dreading the baby, thinking about her overdraft and wondering whether it was better to be worrying about her overdraft or worrying about the difficulties of being an unmarried mother. She never once thought about losing Timothy. She felt as if she had entered one of the novels she read. The rainbow, soapsud world. Losing Timothy became a dramatic possibility to be resolved in the final chapter.

She never got beyond the prologue in that particular novelette. In a week she rang the doctor.

"I don't know whether to be glad or sorry," said the doctor. "The test was negative."

"Does that mean I'm not pregnant?"

Timothy was sitting beside her, smoking. He winced. Did she have to choose this, of all moments, to indulge her perpetual childishness.

The phone crackled. "Oh, thank God," said Joanna, and Timothy wondered what *that* meant. She put down the phone and hugged him.

"I'm not, it's all right." For the moment that she had had to wait for the doctor's explanation had destroyed her dramatic mood and released her to the fears of reality. She couldn't bear to lose Timothy. Having a baby meant losing Timothy. At least she obeyed the inexorable ersatz logic of her novelettes. If you make an emotional sacrifice you go through with it. You give the married man back to his boring wife. You return him to his dreary semi. You sit alone with the record-player amongst the straw-covered Chianti bottles and you weep for him, but you do make the sacrifice. Joanna looked around the flat. At least there would have been no Chianti bottles.

Timothy was relieved into a kind of ecstatic affection. He'd never felt so fond of Joanna as he did now that he needn't be tied to her. Ever since he'd taken his first job he'd hated *having* to do things. Having to get up, having to shave, having to eat. He'd often wished that bodies didn't require food. It would save so much time. He didn't enjoy food the way Joanna did. She actually liked gnawing chicken bones and chewing gristle. She was even capable of eating fish bones and apple cores. It bored and wearied him to disentangle an edible portion from a bony fowl. To spit a discreet fish bone into a white handkerchief. That is, if he could ever *find* a white handkerchief.

So Timothy was living with Joanna because he didn't

have to marry her, and Joanna, grieving both for her lost baby and for her lost role, started another novelette in her head.

One night in bed she asked Timothy to marry her. He thought she was joking until she burst into tears.

"But why?" he asked.

"Because I'd like to have your child and I never want to be like that again. Worried like that. I knew that week I'd have to lose you in order to have the baby. I want to *choose* to have the baby."

It was true, but Joanna was really afraid that Timothy would leave her. Because she loved him and marriage seemed too important for flattering deceits, she told him this.

"And I'm afraid you'll leave me. If you leave me now I'll be OK. I'll get over it." Joanna was well acquainted with Timothy's dislike of chicken bones.

"But unless something happens now, unless we either get married or split up the whole thing will just peter out."

Ah yes, thought Timothy, gone that first fine careless rapture. He knew what was happening now, an event.

"I couldn't."

"All right. I'm going."

And Joanna got out of bed and packed her suitcase.

"Please stay."

"No."

"I'll think about it."

Well, what could he do. He was living in Joanna's flat and he had no job. He'd been living on Joanna's allowance and he had no money. As he looked at Joanna's stocky legs bent over the suitcase he thought of Joanna's affection, easily spilling over him.

"That's not enough," said Joanna, staggering with her suitcase towards the door.

"Joanna."

"What?"

"Please stay."

When Joanna saw the trace of tears on his cheek she knew that she would stay as surely as he now knew that he would marry her.

As Joanna lay in bed, wiping the salty smear of mascara from her cheeks, she thought of that time. She had been unforgivable. If she had allowed him even to *seem* to make up his own mind, even to *seem* to ask her to marry him, she might have been forgiven. It was a token of her very real love for him that she hadn't written a better script. She'd needed him too much for that and that was unforgivable.

# A Child Is Born

THE GRASS lay, like hay, across the shorn lawn, in great golden drifts. Light streamed through the high Georgian rooms of the flat and Joanna felt utterly content, for the day before the doctor had told her that she was, as she had suspected, expecting a baby. They'd just moved into this flat which seemed so much more solid than the shabby rooms they'd had, perched high over Dublin's rooftops. Joanna had thought that flat very picturesque in her time. The time of student parties and extravagance when time hadn't mattered very much. You ate when you felt like it, and you stayed in bed all morning if you felt like that too. The only limit to time, the only time time was timed in those days, was in late Summer when the September exams loomed, marking off another year of timeless time.

Well, it was September again and Joanna was waiting for the baby with more joy and content than she had thought it was possible to fall to her lot. She had been in the habit of thinking of herself as unfortunate, though she had been more fortunate than most people. She had had a happy and interesting childhood. An adolescence that she had shadowed for herself in a misery of self-pity and indignation. Her time at University had been ridden with uneasy, contrived love affairs. That is, Joanna had contrived the love affairs and they had been uneasy because no amount of artistic endeavour will create love. So she hadn't been loved, or not in the way she had wanted to be loved.

Joanna was aware that she was fortunate and she often wondered why she was unhappy, why she pitied herself so much. Perhaps it was because so many things in her life had turned out not to be as they seemed. The certainties of her childhood world had been shattered by divorce. She had thought her parents loved each other and she had gradually discovered that they did not. She had thought that she was exceptionally gifted and, for years, she had failed exam after exam. She had thought that she was beautiful. As a child she had gazed at her unformed reflection with love. But the features had formed, and formed, alas, was the word. Joanna sometimes comforted herself that she had *strong* features. At other times, when she had looked in the mirror, she would beat her head with a hairbrush.

Now in her contentment Joanna was prepared to settle for less. So the present wasn't as exceptional as the past had promised. She hadn't had a brilliant college career but she had, at last, passed her exams. She knew she wasn't beautiful but neither was she plain. She hadn't had a great love affair, but she *had* married and her marriage was happy. If she suspected at times that Timothy didn't love her, she was always sure that he liked her. One of the closest bonds between them was the half-expressed knowledge both felt that, in marrying each other, they had settled for less. They sometimes talked to each other about their past, and of course unhappy, love affairs. Such conversations induced in them both an excited affection. They each felt flattered that the other had been loved, had loved, at some other time.

Joanna went out to the garden and began to gather up the sheaves of cut grass. She felt heavy and clumsy and bending had already become a problem. Her back ached slightly but she was pleased by all these symptoms. She had suspected that she might be pregnant for three long summer months before she had gone to the doctor. She had been sure that nothing as normal as that could happen to her. Many of her friends, her women friends, felt the same way. One of them had said, "I feel like that. It does seem incredible. Why, I don't know. I mean, obviously we must all be biologically capable of it. But it seems such an unlikely sort of thing to be able to do when you can't even mend an electric light plug." As if in an increasingly plastic world, women should melt inside and babies arrive in glossy packets. Stamped 5 lbs 6 oz. Small but tender. Joanna wondered whether women had felt less surprised by conception when they'd had to bake their own bread, even when bread was still sold wrapped in brown paper.

Anyway, now she knew, though she still found it difficult to believe. Her thickening body and her aching back had not belied her. Those three months she'd thought that perhaps she wasn't pregnant at all, that she was just blowing up, and would burst, presently, like a gas balloon. She felt proud of her aches and pains as she raked the grass slowly into a heap at the side of the lawn.

She heard the back door rattle and Timothy ran quickly down the steps into the garden. He looked rushed, as if he was on his way to do something and hadn't arrived home yet.

"Hi," she said.

"Hi, Joanna. I'm afraid I've some rather bad news. Jane's baby has German measles."

So it wasn't all right after all. She might have known that something would go wrong. That her baby, scarcely realised, would be threatened.

"Timothy, can you remember when we saw the baby? I mean I kissed it. Oh blast, this *would* happen." She actually felt a petulant rage against fate for spoiling her fun again like this.

"We saw the baby last week. Look Joanna, don't worry, we'll go to the doctor. There's something, surely, they can do. There's a rabbit serum, I'm almost sure."

"You don't think he'll say I should get rid of it, do you? I couldn't bear that. I mean, say I got rid of it and there was nothing wrong with it, after all." Joanna already believed that it was very unlikely that nothing would be wrong with the baby.

"No, he won't let you get rid of the baby, that's certain.

55

There's no abortion here anyway, not even for health reasons."

Joanna felt relieved. At least she needn't lose her baby yet.

They went to the doctor who gave Joanna the serum. The doctor told them that they could, in fact, find out whether the baby was at risk and he took a sample of blood from her to test. He would give them the results of the test in a week.

That week separated Joanna and Timothy, for Joanna was so frightened that she could scarcely talk to him. She couldn't bear to name and expose her fears. She was afraid that he would be unable to quiet them. She was afraid that if she talked of them, her fears would become more real.

And babies are supposed to bring people together thought Timothy. He was kind to her. He brought her cups of coffee and asked her how she was. But it is impossible to reassure someone who thinks they have a fatal disease. You know they don't, you know how unlikely it is that that pain in the arm presages a stroke, but the fearful sufferer thrusts away comfort, knowing that it's easy to be reassuring about someone else's body. Joanna felt like that. Oh, she knew that it was Timothy's baby too, but when the baby was threatened she couldn't think of it as *their* baby. It was her baby, in her body, and he could be as reassuring as he liked but he wasn't tormented by her doubt. She doubted if her inadequate body could protect the baby enough and carry him safely out of danger.

In a week they knew that the baby was safe and the hideous visions of a blind helpless baby, or, worse still, a vacant mindless child quietened in Joanna's thoughts.

When the danger had passed Timothy's tolerance gave way. Joanna said one evening as they sat drinking coffee in the firelight, "I'm so relieved. You don't know what it was like. I was so frightened."

"Of course I bloody well know what it was like. It's my baby too, isn't it. You know perfectly well that I'd mind much more than you would if that baby was an idiot. Don't you? Well, don't you?"

He *would* have minded terribly. He was very proud and rather amused that he was going to be a father. He was happy to walk beside Joanna's billowing form as the father of the baby inside her. It had been difficult to reassure her in that week of silence and abstraction, when he had been able to trace and echo her visions. If the child had been born blind or an idiot, Joanna would have coped. Women, and especially Joanna, were like that. She would have accepted it but Timothy could not have borne it. Pride and amusement changing into shame and fear. He would have been ashamed of the shame. One shouldn't be ashamed of one's own baby even if it is an idiot, though one should be proud of its intelligence if it is intelligent.

"I know you would have minded," said Joanna resentfully. "You would have been ashamed."

"Yes, I would. It's not unnatural."

"No, I suppose not." She did think it was unnatural. Why ashamed, of all unlikely responses? Fear, yes, but shame, no. It wasn't as if it was his fault, after all.

They were both still warily happy. Joanna began to attend the clinic, which she hated, but it made her feel normal, if somewhat unimportant. She disliked the queues of tired blown women with their weary talk of other children. They'd all *had* other children. She disliked the glossy green walls and the hospital smell. She disliked the contemptuous doctor who never let her ask questions. He just weighed her and felt her and told her to take her vitamin pills. She grew larger and distances stretched. A short walk became a long walk and miles became leagues. Timothy got used to her pregnancy, her aches and her pains. The time seemed much shorter to him than it did to her. After all, it was her body.

The year wheeled towards Christmas and Joanna went into town to shop. She felt exhilarated and happy again as she walked along the wet, sparkling street. There were lights and gold paper in the shop windows. There was a flurry of excitement and joy in the breathless voices of the carol singers who were stamping their feet on the cold pavement. Really, she thought, perhaps having a baby *will* be exciting. The clinic, the early fears, had seemed to reduce this event to a dreary commonplace. It was ages since she had felt excited about it. At least, she thought, it certainly does seem real. Nothing could be as real as that chilly clinic, full of brisk questions and exhausted replies.

As Joanna waited to cross the busy road a car braked, slid and crashed with great force into a lamp post. The carol singing died and a crowd gathered around the car in a quiet, murmuring rush. When the crowd parted to make a path for an authoritative little man with an attache case, Joanna could see a woman's body, rigid against the steering wheel. There was broken glass and blood all over the woman's yellow curls. Joanna stood where she was, transfixed like the woman against the steering wheel. The doctor came away from the car shaking his head.

"She's gone I'm afraid."

When Timothy came home that evening he found the flat in darkness. Joanna was sitting in a chair near the window.

"Joanna what's wrong?"

He turned on the light and saw her there, tears pouring quietly down her cheeks. She wasn't sobbing so he knew it was serious this time.

"I'm so frightened. I just saw a woman killed in a car crash and I'm so frightened."

"That's horrible, but you've nothing to be frightened of. We don't use the car."

"It's not that. It's just that she was dead. It was awful. All blood and glass, and then I came home here and it was all quiet and dark and no life anywhere and I tried to think about the baby. You know the clothes and the cot were delivered today. So I unpacked those but I kept thinking of what you said when I got furious about having to wait so long like this for the baby. You said that it was inevitable that the baby should be born."

"Well, it *is* inevitable," said Timothy. "Quite."

"Yes, I know, but all I could think of after today and that crash was — so is my death."

"Don't, Joanna. That kind of panic goes away, you know. You'll just find that you'll stop thinking about it. Don't swallow up all the joy in the baby in a panic about death."

Joanna couldn't help it. She tried to find things to do with her time. She thought about redecorating the flat. But she was so heavy and clumsy that it was difficult for her to walk far now, never mind paint. She spent evenings in her chair by the window watching the lighted windows of the house at the end of the garden. Sometimes a woman came and stood beside the window and brushed her hair in front of the mirror there. This cheered Joanna because she felt that if the woman could stand there, so normal and unaware of her doom, then the panic was abnormal. Then she would think that the panic was, after all, about something real, that was going to happen, inevitably, and she'd clutch the sides of her chair and shake.

It was very hard on Timothy. He wasn't amused any more. He resented her. He knew she was frightened and lonely but it was so like her. They'd got over the first hurdle, the measles scare, and now instead of anything as normal as being frightened of actually having the baby, she'd gone off at a tangent. Frightened of the inevitable. You couldn't tell her the inevitable wasn't. Whoever heard of evitable. She had always suspected promise and hope and now she'd put herself beyond them. He wondered if she would ever reconcile herself to life in its tawdry truth, now that she'd come up against death.

Inevitably the baby started to come. Joanna had never been afraid of the process of birth itself and she was shocked by the reality. The humiliating introduction. "Just as if they wanted to shame me," she thought as she lay exhausted, stinging and cramped from the shaving and purging.

Then the pain began and all thought of shame or fear, panic or death went out of her head. The baby was born to a blaze of light and a blare of canned music. The canned music, she had been told, would keep her mind off her sufferings. They showed her the creased hairy little bundle that was her son. As she smiled at his ugly perfection the nurse said, "There you are, you see. The Blessed Virgin intercedes with God to make you forget the pain, you know. And there you are. You've forgotten it already, haven't you." Joanna knew that she would never forget that pain.

An hour later Timothy came to the hospital.

"How are you?"

"I'm fine," she said, "but it was ghastly. I spent all last night being hideously sick in a horrid little bare room with a crucifix on the wall. I felt as if I'd just been laid out and whenever I rang the bell the nurse would come and tell me that I wasn't in labour yet. Do you know what she said? 'You're not getting anywhere,' she said. As if I'd failed her somehow. And then when I got sick all she could say was 'Whiskey. Oh, really, Mrs. Gibbons,' You see, I was nervous when it all started so I thought I'd have a drink before I came in here." She *would* think something like that, thought Timothy, but he thought it with affection.

Although she looked tired and drained, although her body looked almost deprived without its robust curve, she sounded happier, more lively than she had for months.

"Have you seen the baby?" she asked, almost fearfully.

"Oh yes."

"Is he all right?"

"Apart from the fact that he has cauliflower ears and looks like a rather red prize fighter, he's all right."

Joanna had no sense of humour. Certainly not about this.

"What's wrong with his ears?"

"Nothing. They just look like cauliflowers, that's all. I promise you he's fine."

"Oh thank God."

She sounded happy again and Timothy began to realise what had happened to her. Life, however tawdry, is a precious gift to hand on.

# Losing

ANNE WOBBLED towards the kitchen and put the kettle on. She filled a glass and crumpled two damp, fuzzy Alka Seltzer tablets into the water. Her head throbbed. Her mouth felt as if it had been scrubbed out with Vim so she lit herself a cigarette to justify the taste. She used to enjoy Jonathan's parties so much. She never used to feel like this the morning after them. In the early days he hadn't trusted her with the cleaning up. He used to get a woman in, someone who could handle his precious antiques. She'd been so young then and enchanted. He'd been enchanted too by her youthful clumsiness.

"Funny little thing, aren't you. Wouldn't let you near a brass coal scuttle, never mind a crystal decanter."

He used to deal in antiques and when the boom in antiques faltered, the great carved furniture had settled uneasily in the large quiet flat. It was an attic flat with low ceilings and a row of south facing windows. The deep velvet plums and pinks and Wedgewood greens seemed to absorb the light, and the Persian carpet, a bargain that no one seemed to appreciate, obscured the wooden floor which used to shine redly in the afternoon light.

Anne poured the boiling water over instant powder in her mug. He'd never bothered much with the kitchen. It was a little dark hole beside the bathroom with an ancient, sticky gas stove. She'd tried to clean the stove once but black gunge stuck to her fingers and she'd given it up. She liked cooking but he was happier in restaurants. Restaurants were good for business. When he wasn't making contacts he liked to relax beside the coal effect electric fire with a Chinese take-away and a fat American novel about cars, or hospitals, or hotels, but most of all about sex.

Anne staggered into the sitting room and groped her way through the antiques and empty glasses. She pulled back the heavy crushed velvet curtains and light filtered through the stale smoky air. She opened a window and leaned out. There was a soft rainy breeze and rushes of damp sunny air rustled the blossoms in the park beneath her. It was Spring. It was a long time since she had noticed the seasons much. You noticed Christmas because it was the height of party time and parties were good for business. She'd noticed recently that the parties themselves didn't seem to be important. The important bit was meeting in the pub beforehand. There was a clutch of pubs in the narrow streets around Grafton Street. They were all very much the same. Comfortable, expensive and crowded. Full of loud voices and business deals.

It started to rain with gentle determination so Anne shut the window and went to see if there was any post. There was. She opened her letter with shaking fingers. She'd been accepted as English and History teacher in a small Protestant school.

She remembered the interview. "Why do you want this job, Miss Connell? I always ask, you know. I find it interesting to find out what you young girls are looking for in a place like this. It's a small school, you know, and when a teacher is ill we expect the others to rally around. Rather gruelling sometimes. And you must know there's nothing glamorous about teaching." This with a look at Anne's leather embroidered coat.

"Oh I like teaching, and a small school, well, you can get to know the pupils better." Better than the jostling drinking crowds. A small school is a safe place. There's nothing as certain as quiet rows of desks, and the dusty smell of chalk.

Anne was writing the third copy of her letter of acceptance when Jonathan came home "to grab a

62

sandwich."

"Still feel awful?"

"No, not now." It was true. She felt dazed and weak but better than she had felt for a long time.

"I've been accepted. I've got the job. I'm to start in September. Isn't it marvellous?"

She rarely had anything exciting to tell him, while his life was a continual explosion of events. Her excitement had made her careless.

"But what about the dating thing? I thought you were going to help. You said you would. You know it starts in September."

Well, she *had* said she would help. She hadn't really thought she would be accepted and her life with Jonathan had seemed more real than the years at college – the scraped degree that she had managed to cling on long enough to achieve. The teaching diploma had been undertaken in the same spirit that some women do charity work. Just to pass the time when Jonathan was too busy to see much of her. To give her something to do when he was out on a deal. But somehow the quiet, necessary hours in the classroom and the soothing respect of the polite little Protestant girls had lured her into taking herself almost seriously at last.

"I know I said I'd help. But you don't really need me. You can get someone else."

That, though, made her hesitate. He *would* get someone else. Probably another girl and what would happen then. But after all, they'd been together now for five years. Surely their relationship would survive.

"But that's not the point, is it?" He took off his jacket and sat down on a green velvet wing chair. "The point is that you said you'd do it. You *committed* yourself to it."

"Oh Jonathan, really. You can't *commit* yourself to a computer dating business."

He was offended. "I don't see why not. It's a job. It provides a service for lonely people. It allows them to meet each other without embarrassment. You don't have to be snobbish about it."

One of the qualities Anne had always admired in Jonathan was his capacity for believing his own propaganda. If his ideas had been less ephemeral he might have been a rich man by now. As it was, he never lost money and usually made quite a bit.

"I'm not being snobbish. But you can find someone else." Again that stirring of fear. "And I'm really just hanging on the outside of your life. They're your ideas, your money, your friends you deal with. I want something of my own."

His light eyes flickered over her face.

"Look, I've always said you should have something of your own. God, I paid for your teaching course. I've seen you sitting there in the pub yawning and wishing it was closing time. That's not the point. You'll never be able to do anything properly until you learn to stop messing about. You committed yourself to one job. You've got to do it. Meet your first commitments first."

So that was it. The work ethic. Prior commitments first. Do a job well, however worthless the job.

"I can't. I've got to take this job. I'll help in the evenings."

"I'm warning you, Anne. If you let me down over this, then we're finished. Right now."

"Oh don't be silly."

She looked at him. He was leaning forward in his chair. His dark hair had just been cut but it still curled over his ears. His fingers gripped each other. He wasn't being silly. He meant it.

"You can't mean that. We've been together for five years."

"Oh I mean it all right. Look —" making it easier for her — "I need you for this. I can't pay someone. It would make the whole thing astronomical to set up. I need someone who'll work long hours for half nothing and who knows me and the way I work. You'll get money in the end of course. I've even been thinking of offering you a limited partnership."

She looked at him with suspicion. She knew that he could pay someone, easily, with the money he spent on her alone in a casual evening in a pub. He'd never offered her partnership, limited or otherwise, before. He knew how she'd longed to marry him. He'd joked about it. "Longing for domesticity in a semi, are you?" Now that she came to think of it, most of his friends' wives did live in far-flung semis. They never came to the pubs. They stayed at home, night after night, with their children, and waited for their wheeling, dealing husbands.

"Perhaps I wouldn't have liked to marry you after all."

"I told you you wouldn't." He leant back in his chair and stretched. "I can be right you know."

"You're not right about my job, you're right for you but not for me. I've got to do it."

He stood up and crossed to the cocktail cabinet, the one piece of modern furniture in the room.

"Well, you know where I stand." He didn't bother to plead with her any more He was quite sure she'd give in. As Anne realised this, recognised this, she was almost sure that she *would* give in. She always had. Over marriage. Over the nights in the pubs. She'd learned to arrange herself like a chair for him to sit in. She began to wonder if he wasn't getting just a bit too heavy.

"Can I have a drink?"

"Sure."

As he poured it she looked down at her crumpled letter of acceptance. She'd squeezed it in her hand when he'd reminded her about the computer dating. Computer dating, indeed. It was terrifying really. How she'd almost believed in it, seen it as he saw it. Providing a service. A service for lonely people. He hadn't even cared when she'd woken in the night with a bad dream. She'd often woken him in her panic. "Ah, go back to sleep. It's only a bad dream." She had one particular very bad dream. It recurred. She dreamt she was about to be executed and that she was begging him not to let them do it. She knew,

65

in the dream, that he could stop them. He'd take her arm and lead her to the sharp shining instrument that was going to remove her head. He'd put his arm around her to comfort her as he drew her nearer and nearer her doom. "It must happen," he'd say. "It's got to be done. The machine must be used today." Oh it was a ridiculous dream but it always left her drained and depressed the next day. As if there was something hideous that she'd forgotten about and would shortly remember. She'd never been able to tell him what the dream was. It was so ridiculous. But don't lonely people dream? How can you provide a service for them if you don't understand their dreams?

"Will you really finish it, Jonathan, if I take the job?" He handed her a drink and lit himself a cheroot.

"Yes, I mean it."

"I've never let you down before." She sipped her drink. She felt numb, but pleasantly so.

"Every time you yawned in the pub you let me down. Every time you implied that my work had no value. Oh you let me down all right. You and your secret superiority. You *were* superior. You sneered at me and my job. I often thought you envied me. You'd never have the nerve to make money. You'd need to know that you had a degree in something and a certificate of moral worth from your intellectual friends before you'd even *earn* money."

"All right. I'm going to take the job." She waited. She already knew the answer.

"Take it then and get out." He ran into the bedroom and came back carrying her suitcase. "Here you are. Fill it yourself. Go on, pack. Just get out of here now." A fine hail of saliva misted the air. "You've let me down. You're getting out of here."

One of his oldest friends had once got a contract for supplying Georgian furniture to an hotel. It was a contract Jonathan had coveted. She'd come back from her lectures and found him lying, face downwards, on their bed.

"Jonathan, Jonathan what's wrong?" she'd asked. He'd looked up. His face was red. It shone and at first she thought he'd been crying.

"What's wrong?"

"That fucking bastard," he shouted, "he's taken my contract." He'd put his head back on the pillow and groaned.

He couldn't bear to lose.

# Pieces of Silver

"I SAID don't do that!"

"Do what?"

He had wrapped a piece of plastic around the poker and it was spluttering and gasping in the sitting room fire. She might heat up fish fingers night after night, but they *did* have a sitting room fire. Like families on television. Daddy, Mummy and their two tiresome coy children all gazing dutifully into their Bord na Móna fire. But Andrew wasn't dutiful.

"I said don't do that!"

He looked at her and bent his thin bare neck over the little pile of plastic pieces beside him on the hearth rug. He took the hot poker out of the fire and waved it over the grate. It was smoking and it smelled terrible. Then he dropped pieces of plastic onto the cooling poker and wrapped them carefully around it until it was a rancid, erupting black pudding. Then he drove it back under the cinders.

"Oh God, don't!"

"Do what?"

But she slumped back in the chair and lit another cigarette. Her glass shone in the light as she drank from it. For a moment he'd hoped she was going to hit him.

She wished she even wanted to hit his silly resentful face. She *had* wanted to, for a moment. But it never lasted, that kind of feeling with her now. She could always have another cigarette or another sip. Never too much or too quickly, mind you. She rationed her drink and her cigarettes. She'd been careful since John died. She kept the household going anyway. She couldn't cook, not for a child, and she wasn't really interested in eating herself, but when Andrew came home from school his favourite meal was waiting for him. Five neat fish fingers and two tomatoes, for vitamins and things. Fish fingers were protein after all and she remembered how she used to pride herself on serving fresh food. But John wasn't here to insist on homegrown vegetables and the vegetable garden was overgrown now anyway and fresh vegetables were expensive in the shops.

The plastic flared and crackled in the fire.

"It's time you went to bed."

He poked the turf and light flecks of ash swirled around the grate.

"Please Andrew, you're old enough to behave a bit better than this."

"Will you come?"

She got up, wishing that she didn't have to. She was so tired all the time now. Maybe she was ill. She didn't feel ill. She just felt tired at the thought of doing any of the things she had to do. Getting up or going to bed. The only time she felt comfortable was when she was sitting in front of the fire on her own. When Andrew had gone to bed and she could sit there with the last of her drink, smoking, while the neat briquettes concertinaed untidily in the dying fire.

"I'll come."

She used to enjoy putting him to bed. He was an only child and she was so delighted with him that every chore was a ritual, bathing him – she called it "bathing the baby" – dressing him and reading to him in bed at night. His dependence enchanted her and she prolonged it greedily. "You're spoiling my son," John had said with a sigh but he hadn't really interfered. He had been ill since Andrew was a baby and he'd left his wife and son alone in their kindergarten world. Alone, but Harriet hadn't felt lonely, she'd felt safe and happy with her feeding formulas and teddy bear mugs and John came home every evening even if he didn't seem very happy about it. Harriet knew she should try to find out why he seemed so indifferent and apart but he was almost savage with her when she asked him what was wrong, had she done anything wrong, was he feeling alright, had he stopped loving her. "Leave me alone," he said and, with a mixture of hurt and guilt, she did leave him alone. She made Andrew her companion.

As Andrew sat up in bed waiting for her to open the book he remembered how she used to talk to him before she opened the book at bedtime. He didn't like being read to at all but he'd always loved listening to her when she curled up at the end of the bed with a book in her lap and a cushion at her back.

"It was cold, you'd never think it could be really cold beside the sea but it was. Freezing. There wasn't even a sea breeze. It was still and cold, almost paralysed. And then it started to snow and the islands floated in the sea like fat polar bears and my little brother was your age then but he wouldn't go home until his hands were red and sore because he said he wanted to watch everything changing." She had a special voice for remembering. The way actors have special voices on the stage. He didn't like actors but he liked listening to her because she used that voice for him, just for him. His father had come in one evening when she was talking before reading time. He came in very quietly and stood in the open doorway and listened. Andrew had been terrified. He hadn't been able to listen to his mother at all. He had clutched onto the warm corner of the pillow where the hot water bottle was and he'd watched his father's face. The voice stopped and she picked up the book and his father's face smiled and he winked at Andrew and crept away. He wasn't always cross. Andrew knew that, but whenever he tried to think of a time when his father hadn't been cross he remembered that time as the only time. Perhaps because that time it was more than not cross, it was as if his father was like them. As if he liked stories. *She* didn't like stories now. She read to him every night   but she never told stories and she had a special humming voice for reading these days. What he called an "And then" voice. And then. And then. And then.

He couldn't remember when it started. The humming voice, the bored voice he called it at the beginning. Whenever he tried to remember it made him feel sick because he saw the night she came in with a bunch of red roses squashed in her hands.

"He was dead when I got there and I couldn't even leave him the roses, he *insisted* on it. Don't leave me any flowers, he said."

"There," said Aunt Emma who didn't tell stories but who stayed in the room until Andrew went to sleep. "There Harriet."

"Where Harriet?" his mother had screamed and she'd begun to laugh and cry and beat against the bed end with her battered roses and Emma had said "There" again and whispered and they'd both looked at Andrew and his mother had hugged him and left the front of his pyjamas damp and then she'd gone with Aunt Emma.

She'd gone. After that there were no stories, just books and no meals with smells, just things to eat. She never ate with him. She never even sat down at the table with him now. She sighed around the kitchen with a cigarette in her mouth, tidying up, and she didn't tell him to eat up his vegetables anymore. She didn't even eat them all up herself when he wouldn't. She used to do that. She was always cross with him for not finishing everything because, she said, it was bad for her diet. And then she'd eat what was left on his plate with her fingers and pretend that the food had just caught in her fingers on the way to the bin.

The room was quite dark and he realised she must have turned out the landing light. She hadn't even come in to say goodnight or turn off his bedside lamp though he was glad he could keep it on now because when he woke up in the night he couldn't run to her. Her room was too far away and there was a little flight of stairs on the way and two dark rooms with open doors just waiting to suck him in. He couldn't run to her but if he woke up he could count the roses on the lampshade until the lampshade didn't work anymore and then it would be day and he could look out his window at the terrace and watch the first people going to work.

Harriet woke up. She'd gone to sleep in front of the fire and she was cold because she'd slept in her clothes. Bone cold as if she'd never get warm again unless she had a hot water bottle and a hot bath. There was no one to insist so she wrapped herself up in a rug and sat in the chair in front of the fire. Well, she'd turned off the landing light and Andrew was asleep when she looked in. Asleep under that hideous lamp that John's mother had given him. Roses. Well, that could have been funny.

"I'm not having it. It's not pretty. Burn me. Do you hear me? Burn me. If you leave flowers anywhere. . . . No flowers."

In the hospital with the cream walls and the doctors who were never there and the nurses who always were. He complained all the time, not of pain or of fear but about the food and the nurses and the colour of the walls. He grumbled like a sick child. He asked her to bring him fruit or wine and when she arrived with a perfect peach or a snipe of his favourite champagne he trembled with frustration.

"It tastes of cotton wool, you never could choose fruit. They saw you coming when they sold you this and the champagne's warm. Where did you put it, on the car radiator?"

"I iced the champagne before I left home, John, and the man told me that the peaches only came in yesterday. Maybe they taste odd because you aren't feeling well."

He agreed in the end. He said he couldn't taste anything and he told her not to bring him anything to eat. She was sorry because at least he had enjoyed complaining but then she realised that he didn't mean to give *that* up.

"I want you to get Dermot White to come in here. As soon as possible, tell him it's urgent and don't let him put you off. You always let people put you off." He closed his eyes. "Tell him to hurry." And Harriet agreed and left the hospital in tears. Her mouth ached. She felt as if no amount of crying would relax her strained throat and she wished she could be simply sorry for John. She was terrified and irritated and she didn't want to get close to him in case he told her what it was like for him, in case he drew her into his nightmare.

He did. He gave his solicitor elaborate instructions for his death. He wasn't interested in making a will. He wanted to design a concrete end, a hard grey wall for Harriet to hit herself against. No flowers, no funeral, not even a memorial service. The body to be given to medical science and cremated privately afterwards. Andrew was to go to school the next day.

"I'm not having you prettying it up. Or making a thing of it. Be bad for the child. Confuse him. Death's a fact and you're not to linger over it or disguise it."

So he died without grace or ease. With no flowers or ceremony to cut off the appalling memory of his dying. And Harriet found it difficult to remember him now as anything other than a dying man. He used to think she was funny. He used to laugh at her because she still read school stories about hearty little girls who wore black stockings and played lacrosse.

"You're so immature," he said coldy a week before he died.

A piece of plastic flared in the fire. Andrew must have hidden it at the back or left it there by accident. She knew she should be more careful with Andrew and she promised herself she'd make an effort tomorrow, but he made her feel tired. Even if she neglected him or read in front of him he made her feel tired. He'd sit there biting his nails while she read and when she looked up from her book she'd find his big hurt brown eyes staring. He'd come home late from school often lately and when this happened she worried in a relieved way. He *said* he was taking football practice but he always looked, well, triumphant when he came in. But maybe he was better at football than he used to be and anyway, as John had said, he was a big boy now. There was no use fussing over him and she must go to bed if she was to get up next morning.

"Mrs. Byrne?"

The telephone had woken her from a late, dream-laden sleep. She felt exhausted.

"Yes?"

"Mrs. Byrne, Gallagher here, Andrew's headmaster. I wonder if you could come over to the school, we've a bit of a problem on our hands."

"Is Andrew sick? Is he hurt? What's wrong?"

"Oh no, it's not that. Nothing like *that*," he said. "No indeed. He's confessed to something. I can't talk about this over the phone," he murmured as if to hoodwink the spies who lurked along the line. "But I think you should be here."

"Confessed? Confessed to what?" It seemed such a ridiculous word. Surely they *owned up* at schools – Andrew was far too young for confessions.

"Better not over the phone, you know. If you'd just come."

The receiver went dead. John had insisted on the school. It was a good school. A good Protestant school with playing fields that were cold and white with frost today. Why hadn't he looked colder when he came home late? The gravel crunched stiffly under her feet as she made her way to the large oak door. She wandered into the entrance hall. Did they always keep the door open? Poor cold boys. And what should she do now, shout or scream, knock at doors or tap a coin against the open door?

"Mrs. Byrne, I was on the lookout. My study looks out to the front, handy for avoiding unwanted parents you know, saving your presence, yes, ah," he added as she looked at him in astonishment. But he wasn't deranged. He was hideously embarrassed.

"Andrew is here, in my study. Come in."

The study was clean and bright and modern. It had been newly decorated in blues and greens. There was a plain fitted carpet and tweed curtains and chair covers. Hariett longed for dust and leather and book lined walls. Andrew was standing by the window. His face was streaked with grimy tears and his clothes were crumpled and untidy. He hadn't seemed untidy at home but maybe she hadn't noticed. And this morning he'd had to get his own breakfast because she'd been asleep.

He didn't move when she came in. He stared out the window.

"Well Andrew, tell your mother what you've just told me."

Mr. Gallagher stood behind his desk as if he felt safer there. Andrew didn't move or speak.

"Andrew, tell me darling. Whatever it is I won't be cross, I promise." She put her arm around him but he hunched his shoulders away from her.

"I stole."

"You what?"

"I stole. Money. From the jackets in the cloakroom. They leave them there when they play football. I stole a bit from each pocket so they didn't notice for a while." He sounded slightly pleased with his ingenuity.

"But darling, I would have given you money. You should have asked me."

He kicked the skirting board with an unpolished shoe. The shoelace was missing.

"Not enough," he muttered.

"Not enough for what, Andrew?"

"The café."

Mr. Gallagher sat down and waved at the chair in front of his desk.

"Do sit down," but Hariett stayed where she was, holding Andrew.

"It seems that Andrew goes to the café, you know the chipper down the road. We all call it the café. He goes there after school. The boys aren't really supposed to go there. Puts them off good school nosh." Mr. Gallagher seemed much happier now that the truth was out. He was almost chirping. "But some of them do go. It's not a rough place so we turn a blind eye to the older ones, but a woman rang up and told me that a small boy went there every evening and she was worried about him. She thought he was too young to be out in the evening. She's a waitress there so it was nice of her to ring," he said thoughtfully. "And the money has been missed. There have been complaints from the boys."

"But why the café? Andrew, why did you want to go there?"

He shrugged. Because it was warm and steamy and noisy. And there were people. The waitress was nice. She always gave him extra chips and told him that he should get on home and not sit there scaring the life out of his Mammy. His Mammy'd be wondering where he was.

"I think Andrew should go back to his class now, Mrs. Byrne." Mr. Gallagher had a *pas devant les enfants* look so Harriet hugged Andrew and watched the door close behind him.

"You see," said Mr. Gallagher, "it's not unusual for, well, let's say a disturbed boy to steal." He looked down at his desk as if he expected to find evidence of this rule there. "Andrew has been very withdrawn since his father died and *you* must have been finding things difficult too of course. Andrew would feel that, you see. He might want to avoid going home. Children don't like grief. They're frightened of it."

Harriet thought she knew what he was saying.

"It was my fault, I neglected him."

"Oh come now, Mrs. Byrne. It was no one's fault. It wasn't Mr. Byrne's fault that he died, was it?" he asked surprisingly. "And this incident follows from that. You must see that."

"Yes, I suppose I do."

"It was very natural that you'd get a bit wrapped up in

yourself after your husband died. You don't have to blame yourself."

She didn't have to but she wanted to. In fact, blaming herself had made her feel better than she had for a long time. It was as if a perfectly useless kitchen utensil like a parsley grater that you never used because you didn't like parsley, had snapped in your hands. She was worn out not blaming herself, exhausted by resisting Andrew's need.

"It *was* my fault," she insisted. "I *did* neglect him. I didn't even see him off to school. And you saw his clothes today, they're a mess. Because I didn't look after him. I didn't even cook him a proper meal in the evening. I ignored him."

Mr. Gallagher sighed. Really, Mrs. Byrne was a most uncomfortable woman. Her face had become quite pink, but then some people had the time to treat guilt and blame as a recreation. Well, he wished she wouldn't waste his. Of course, she was naturally upset, he told himself, he wasn't going to judge her.

"Well, you'd be surprised how many parents neglect their children for less cause. We'll have to punish Andrew a little. But we'll let him off lightly. Extra homework, something like that. And we won't tell the other boys."

"Thank you, that's kind of you."

"Not at all, but perhaps you could return the money, any time you like of course." Widows often found it difficult to raise small sums just like that. "It's five pounds, I think, more or less."

"I have it, I have it here." She opened her handbag and produced various pieces of crumpled tissue, a few spent matches and an open lipstick.

"Oh dear, I *know* my purse is here somewhere."

"It doesn't matter, Mrs. Byrne, you can pay me any time you like." He noticed that her hands were shaking.

"No, I'd like to give it to you now. Here it is," she said, waving the open purse at him as coins clattered across the desk. As she dived after them her handbag fell open onto the floor, scattering pound notes as it went.

"You see," she giggled, "I *knew* I'd be able to pay you back at once."

Harriet waited happily for Andrew that night. She'd spent the afternoon washing and cleaning and cooking. She'd had a lot to do but she didn't feel at all tired. She felt quite intoxicated with her efforts. She was looking forward to making it up to Andrew, she'd offer him a home again. When Andrew came in she went to meet him in the hall and gave him a warm hug to show that whatever he'd done didn't matter.

When the phone rang the next afternoon she was hoovering the stairs.

"Mrs. Byrne?"

"Yes."

"It's most extraordinary, most extraordinary. It seems that I owe you five pounds. I can't understand why he said he did it. Andrew didn't steal at all."

Andrew ran home from school. It was cold but he didn't mind that because everything was different now. She'd talked to him last night the way she used to and she'd cooked him a stew and though she hadn't eaten anything, not even his leftovers, she'd sat down with him at the table. She'd been up and dressed at breakfast and she'd waved goodbye from the door and she'd be waiting for him when he got home.

She opened the door before he knocked and almost pulled him through the door. Her hair was curling around her face instead of being dragged back in her usual greasy pony tail. She looked very pink but not at all pleased.

"Why did you do it, Andrew? You didn't steal at all. One of the teachers caught another boy this afternoon at football practice and he said he'd been doing it all along. Nobody but Mr. Gallagher knew about your silly confession." She shook his shoulders. "Why *did* you do it?"

He wriggled away from her and threw his coat down on

the hall floor.

"I wanted you to pay some attention to me," he shouted. "And you have, haven't you?" and he burst into tears.

"But where did you get the money, then, for the café?" she asked more quietly. She didn't touch him. She couldn't, he'd tricked her.

"From your handbag. I took it as pocket money. You said I could ages ago. You said 'Take what you need. I can't be bothered.'"

"I didn't say 'I can't be bothered.'"

"But you wouldn't pay any attention to me and I didn't know what to do and you didn't even notice when I took the money from your handbag but I thought if Mr. Gallagher told you I was stealing you'd talk to him about me, you know, like in a story." He looked at her. "I mean you like things in stories, don't you?"

# A Matter Of Principle

THE KITCHEN door banged and Geoffrey erupted into the room.

"Don't bang the door, love, you know what your father says. You'll damage the lock."

Jane was tired after a long dreary day of housework. They'd had a dinner party the night before so there was a backlog of cheerless chores that she'd put off in order to cook. Still, it had been a good dinner though she'd felt too tired to talk much. But that had pleased Peter. He'd had a lot to say about the new ecumenical prayer idea. He thought it was a terrible idea.

"If they feel guilty about being Protestants why not abolish the thing altogether. All this kowtowing to Catholics. Shilly-shallying. I always said that school prayers were a ridiculous convention." He had too. "Let their bloody parents teach them to say their prayers. I'm going to put my foot down this time. I'll refuse to attend prayers if they make them ecumenical. Just won't go. It's one thing if they really believe in their own principles. O.K., have proper Protestant prayers. But ecumenical prayers. I mean, God soon won't know who's hollering at him about what."

Jane sighed and stirred the white sauce for the cauliflower. That's what Peter had said last night but she knew that he'd attend prayers, ecumenical or not. It would take a long time, his turnabout. He'd reason himself out of it all the same. He'd make such an issue of it that she'd have to intervene and beg him not to lose his job and she knew that that was what Peter meant her to do.

"Oh, if pennies count more than principles. I sometimes wonder which matters more to you, me or my job." She would be loving with him then and tell him how much she loved and admired him. Then she'd tell him how much the boys would miss him if he left. How valuable his teaching was to the school.

"Oh well, perhaps I have been a bit extreme. It's true that I'm the best bloody teacher in that hell hole, at least I open their eyes a bit. Even used to prevent one or two of them from becoming dear old vicars before their time. Of course none of those boys has the guts to do anything as interesting these days. Don't even believe in their own religion. No wonder. Completely emasculated by all this liberal rubbish."

Jane sometimes wondered why Peter's speech was so abrupt, almost staccato. Perhaps it was because he was his own God and his utterances needed no – well, no *manners* – because they were divine. But divine or not, she could manage him. She managed him by accepting his role as God. It was like pushing someone around in a wheel chair. He was crippled by his own principles but a gentle shove from her could keep him wheeling along. Jane knew that in the end Peter would not only attend the ecumenical payers but think that his presence there was all his own idea.

"Oh I did think of not going, but I couldn't let the boys down. Tear the whole school apart like that. Wouldn't be fair. Besides, if they did sack me, what would happen to the boys?" Of course they wouldn't sack him. Jane knew that but what was the point in being God if you couldn't design your own world. "And what would happen to you and Geoffrey if I got the boot. But you never thought of that, you funny little woman." And he'd stroke her nose in affectionate contempt. Did he really not know that she guided him, or was the affection in fact gratitude and was the contempt for his own weakly held, strongly stated principles. Oh well, it didn't matter anyway. She kept the show on the road and he kept his pride and his principles.

It was just, she thought, as she added cheese to the smooth rich sauce, that it was sometimes so boring. Particularly at the beginning of one of these dramas when she knew exactly what would happen, just what she would have to do to prevent Peter from finding out that no one cared about his principles enough to object to them. It was a bit like reading a recipe and feeling tired at the idea of actually cooking such an elaborate meal.

Geoffrey dipped a finger in the sauce.

"Oh stop that, you great lout. I thought you were doing your homework."

"I'm not."

"I can see that. What *are* you doing then?"

"Getting under your feet." She smiled. Geoffrey made up for a lot.

"Mummy?"

"Yes."

She put the cauliflower in a gratin dish and poured the sauce over it.

"It's my turn to take prayers."

"Well, that's good. It'll make you really feel like a prefect. I'm very proud of you, you know, darling." He blushed. She knew he liked her pride in him. He liked her to have said that she was proud. He hated facing the praise.

"Mummy, they only made me a prefect because of Daddy. You know that."

"Darling, you know your father is a great thorn in their side."

It was an offering. Jane rarely spoke of the difficulties of Peter to Geoffrey but she was tired now and his easy affection and unspoken need had weakened her.

"They wouldn't have made you a prefect to please Daddy."

"I didn't know that you knew he was a thorn. But look, Mummy, it's not simple about taking prayers. I just can't." Jane turned around abruptly and the cheese scattered in little golden grains on the polished floor.

"You can't. Why can't you, for goodness sake?"

"I don't believe all that. I just can't take prayers feeling like that."

"But Geoffrey, Daddy and I don't believe either. It doesn't matter. I mean, Daddy goes to prayers and I go to the occasional school service. It's just a politeness."

"Not for me. Mummy, it's a matter of principle. I just can't."

Jane sat down at the kitchen table. She felt weak. Not this again.

"Oh Geoffrey, haven't we got enough principles?" She was so tired and Peter would expect dinner to be ready and perfect and the sauce had splashed and there was cheese all over the floor.

"Oh I can't bear it." She burst into tears.

"Mummy, I'm sorry." He loomed over her nervously. "Look, you're tired. The dinner and everything," he added knowledgeably. He knew dinners were tiring. She'd often told him so though she'd never mentioned it to Daddy.

"Yes, I'm tired. Oh Geoffrey, can't you really? Couldn't you ask Daddy?"

"You know what he'll say. You always say ask Daddy and he just blusters and does what the school says. Look Mummy, I don't want to be like him, blustering away about principles and then jumping when he's told to. They won't mind at the school, you know. They may have to stop me being a prefect though because taking prayers is one of the duties and Daddy will mind that."

"I didn't know you thought about Daddy like that." She pulled out a packet of cigarettes that she'd been trying not to smoke. Peter hated the smell. He said it was unfeminine.

"Well, I didn't know *you* could cry, did I? And you don't usually smoke. Mummy, you know those toys Daddy used to give me. Those awful Lego things that I kept on losing. I liked one Lego toy, once. And Daddy thought he knew me because of that. So birthday after Christmas and Christmas after birthday he'd give me Lego toys. I hated them. They were so self-conscious and educational. And Daddy would sit down with me and build them with me. 'Exploring the possibilities' he called it. Jesus, those are the only bloody possibilites he knows. He lives in a Lego world, for God's sake, and he's not even good at that. If you didn't lay the foundations the whole damn structure would fall down."

He pushed her relentlessly past limits with his profanity. Peter allowed only Peter to be profane. In other people he called it "inane" or "ignorant". Geoffrey knew that he would have to bully his mother as Peter bullied her if he was to have an ally.

"Goodness," said Jane, "I didn't know that you could talk like that."

"I've been here all the time, you know. It's just that everything here is so limited when Daddy's here. All you ever think of is pleasing him when he's here and that means you make me do it too."

She looked at him. Her great grown up son. She'd been married for seventeen years and she'd built a house of deceit to shield her child. Oh she'd built it for herself as well. But here was her child poking his greasy dark head out through the roof of her neat little house. Cracking away at the tiles and tossing them carelessly in the air. She felt suddenly jubilant. She lit herself another cigarette from the butt of the last.

"What do you want me to do?" The habit of years was strong. She knew a bully when she heard one.

"Tell him I won't take prayers and, well, be on my side."

"You know what he'll be like."

"Oh yes. He won't be able to bear it. But I can and you can. He'll have to put up with a few real principles for a change."

Well, thought Jane as she puffed away happily. It will make a change. With a crisis in the house who can expect cauliflower. Maybe it was wrong to encourage Geoffrey but it made a change from the ordered, exhausting routine.

And after all, she had been trying to protect Geoffrey. That was partly what the order was for.

The kitchen door clanged.

"Well, well, what's this?" Peter mooched in, unwinding his dirty scarf which he put on the kitchen table. He didn't like disorder. He expected Jane to put it away for him.

"God, what a pong," he said, dispersing the lazy wreaths of cigarette smoke. "Is dinner ready? I'm starving."

"No," said Jane. "It's not ready. We have a crisis."

"But I'm starving."

"Well, you'll just have to wait, that's all," said Jane calmly. She was surprised at how easy it all was.

"Geoffrey says he won't take prayers. It's his turn to take them. He says he can't because he doesn't believe. He says he won't. He says it's a matter of principle."

Peter sat down.

"Well, he says, does he? Why doesn't he say it himself then? Eh? What's wrong with his principles if he can't speak for himself?"

Geoffrey backed towards the door. He despised his father but he was afraid of him.

"He's afraid you'll bully him."

"Afraid I'll bully him. So well he might be. What does he think I'm going to do? Tell the headmaster that my privileged little son has too many principles to have the ordinary good manners to take prayers, to fulfil a certain obligation he took on when he became a prefect. Oh no, I'm not going to do that."

"You don't have to," said Geoffrey. "I'll tell him." Peter's sneer and his mother's calm had encouraged him.

"Don't be ridiculous, Peter," said Jane. "He won't need you to speak for him. He's grown up now you know." Though she'd only noticed it that afternoon.

"Oh, grown up. He'll be making love to his mother next I suppose."

Geoffrey shivered.

"This time," said Jane energetically, "you've broken even your own febrile rules. God. You've talked about principles and here's your son, *your* son and thank heavens mine too, and he's got a principle and what do you do? You reduce the whole thing to your own terms. Sentimental. Love. How much do you think that I really love you? How long do you think I would have put up with your boring principles? Nursing them, planting them out, pruning them, except for a principle. A principle I've kept and held for seventeen years. A principle I've loved. That's the difference. I love and hold to my principles. You flirt with yours. There's nothing cheap about my love for Geoffrey, so don't think you can embarrass it, you old goat, with your Freudian garbage. Get back to your little dolly bird of a school secretary. I read that letter she wrote last week. Leonine head indeed." She screamed, "Can't you see that all you are is a greedy fat worm living off my ideas of civilisation."

Geoffrey banged the door behind him.

Peter stood up.

"I can't stand this," he said. He wiped his eyes with the back of his hand. "I'll go and see the boy. If that's the way you both feel, all right. I'll speak to the headmaster. I'll do whatever you want. Don't think I'll enjoy doing it though. But I'll do it."

Jane listened to his stumbling feet on the stairs. The exhilaration had gone. She felt sick. She picked up the gratin dish and scraped the cauliflower into the sani can. She waited in the kitchen, smoking nervously. The smell of the cigarette nauseated her so she stubbed it out and looked with disgust at the crumpled dirty butt in the ashtray.

# The Wedding Party

WE ARRIVED late. I felt pleased with myself. Andrew hadn't been able to get away from work before eleven and so we'd arranged to meet at a bus stop and go to the wedding party together. Actually there was no "so" about it. In earlier headier days I would have gone to the party early and alone. An invitation in myself. By the time Andrew arrived I would have been a walking impersonation of the working man's burden. Drunk and flirtatious. An idle wife defeating her husband's honest endeavour. It wasn't my fault, after all, that he worked at night.

It was different now. I'd done a brisk stocktaking of each one's separate investments in this marriage of ours and I found myself wanting. Andrew had invested money – "I used to be able to survive on five pounds a week before I married you," – time – "I *need* time, just to potter, but you make me account for every minute. Apparently my time is wasted if it's spent away from you." I had invested nothing unwillingly. I wanted to give anything I gave and in the face of his great reluctance I thought it was time that I gave a few unwilling gifts myself.

So we met at a bus stop, under an umbrella in the pouring rain and I thought that to meet like this, face to face late at night in the rain, was a rare and loving thing for a married couple to do. Andrew was pleased to see me, proud to escort me to the party, and when we arrived late and sober when everyone else was merry and tired we felt superior.

We got a bit of a shock though when, drinkless and

sober, we had to join the merrymakers. Andrew went in search of wine — a search which was a habit with him at parties. The honourable way of deserting the drunken wife.

"I'd *like* to be proud of you. Do you think I like it when someone comes and tells me you've passed out. You must realise that when we go to a party together you're my responsibility. I can't enjoy myself if I have to keep an eye on you."

It wasn't going to be like that this time. I'd changed. On the basis of two weeks holiday away from him in the sun, I'd changed. I'd missed him dreadfully. My missing was indeed full of dread. Of shaking limbs and a revolted stomach. The sun gave me a headache and scenic drives gave me vertigo and I knew that the plane would crash before I could get back to Andrew. I would never go on a holiday without him again. I knew now how much I valued him and how lucky I was to have him. I'd behaved badly but I'd behave better in future.

That was all very well but I needed a drink. I didn't know anyone and I'm not the kind of person who looks enigmatic standing on my own at a party. I look frantic. I *feel* frantic. And now I needed a drink to stop my hands from shaking so that I could have a cigarette. It was an awkward party anyway. The floor was strewn with the kind of girls you don't expect to find on floors. Neat girls with well prepared faces and casual hairstyles sitting in circles. They probably worked together. They were talking with great animation and occasional bursts of giggles as they looked over their shoulders to make quite sure that someone would see how much they were enjoying themselves. I didn't want to give them that satisfaction so I glanced away with an assured little smile and found a man smiling back at me.

"Hello," he said. He was slightly drunk. "I know you. I've seen you before. You were standing on the stairs of your house. I was collecting a friend from there and the door was open. I liked you."

I was delighted. I waited anxiously for more.

"I've heard a lot about you too," he said, "from little people who don't like the sort of things you do."

"Like drinking too much and smoking too much, I suppose, and behaving badly at parties."

That was the sort of thing I used to say. Before I changed. I used to think it was honest of me not to desert my past, until Andrew had pointed out that I didn't have to shove it down people's throats. "It doesn't," Andrew had said, "sound enticing. It sounds like a threat."

"You're very unsure of yourself, aren't you?" said my party friend, giving the lie to Andrew. "I like your eyes but your mouth does strange things."

I bit my lip. "Well, I've just come here. I'm sober, stone cold sober," I added with pride. "You'd expect to be tense."

"Yes, I suppose so. But I've a feeling that you're not like you seem at all. I mean you look a bit frigid. But then there's your eyes. *They're* not frigid. Maybe you'd be passionate if you knew how. Maybe you *are* passionate but you just haven't felt it yet."

I was delighted. Andrew had often told me that it was only my startling behaviour that prevented me from being universally admired but I'd always suspected that he just said this to punish me for behaving badly. A sort of more-in-sorrow-than-in-anger rebuke that would leave me mourning my missed opportunities. But it seemed that he was right. Here I was, a sober success.

"Certainly I've felt passionate," I said. "I'm very happily married."

"Oh, marriage," he waved it away. "I'm sure you didn't have much experience before you were married. Of passion, I mean."

I knew what he meant and though I felt this conversation was distinctly improper, I didn't want him to know that. I felt he'd despise prudery and I could see Andrew watching us from the corner of the room, with two wine glasses in his hands.

"Yes, I did," I said firmly. "But I didn't enjoy it much. I just felt that you had to sleep with people to get them to love you."

"You should love people you sleep with, you know."

"Oh I don't know. Animals do it, after all."

I wasn't telling the truth but I wanted to flirt and hurt and not care. I wanted to dissolve pearls in wine and drive sane men crazy, particularly Andrew.

"I'm Paul, by the way, I must have another drink but please stay there. I want you to be there when I get back."

"Oh yes," I said. I had had no intention of moving but I was amazed that he should want to make sure of me. And he did come back but the party shifted and moved around us and Andrew and Paul's wife, Sally, were included in the sparkle of our flirtation.

"Come to lunch," I said, for I liked his wife on sight.

"We'd love to."

"Come on Sunday. I hate Sundays. Lunch is about the only thing you can do with Sundays."

"Well, we'd like to come if we can find a babysitter for the children," said Sally. "We'll let you know."

"How many children do you have?"

"Three."

"Bring them," I said airily. I had a nasty feeling that I was going to regret this. Sausages for the children, orange squash, and could we really afford to give anyone lunch? Particularly on Sunday. We generally run out of money on Saturday evening and empty the phone coinbox on Sunday morning. Also you can't really flirt with a half of a married couple with three children. At least I can't. It's one thing to drive sane men crazy and quite another to try to make nice women jealous. And Sally was nice. She had a gentle face that looked as if it had been very thoroughly cleaned of all pretence. Well, it was a pity about the flirtation, particularly as Andrew still looked calm and even proudly loving. As if he was glad that his wife had managed to have a little innocent fun and enjoy a little flattery. He was probably glad I'd made so few demands.

Lunch loomed and I clattered nervelessly around the kitchen sipping cider and dropping forks on the floor. Andrew was laying a table for the children in the garden because he doesn't like children making noisy demands either. The glasses were smeared and I couldn't make them sparkle because the glass cloth had been used to clean the egg off the floor. The knives and forks *looked* clean to me but I washed them again because the last time we had people to lunch Andrew had noticed a gritty fork in the middle of the meal. So I clattered and sipped and sipped, alas, too much.

"Goodness," said Paul when he and his family arrived. "Goodness, you're squiffy."

"She wouldn't say that," said Andrew gently. "She likes to say she's tired."

"Well, lunch is ready," I snapped. "Andrew, do pour a little wine." Andrew thinks it's crude to fill up wine glasses to the brim. I was hurt and cross and I couldn't get lunch on the table fast enough. I knew that if you made yourself squiffy, drunk or tired, you shouldn't really be surprised if someone calls attention to the fact. But you don't have to like them for it and you certainly don't want to loiter around drinking with them.

"We're thinking of separating," said Paul chattily as I served the chicken. The children were shrieking around the garden.

"Oh," I said thoughtfully, removing cigarette ash from a chicken leg. "Oh, I see." I didn't see at all.

"Yes," said Sally. "I'm sick of ignoring his little dollies wherever I go. Perhaps I wouldn't mind if I didn't always know about his affairs." She paused and thought about it.

Andrew poured wine into an overflowing wine glass and I opened and shut the oven door. I admired her candour but there seemed so many wrong things to say in reply.

"This latest affair is the worst, I think. It keeps going on and on. Usually they don't last but this one has. I've told him that if he doesn't give her up I'll leave him, and he won't so we're separating. The chicken is delicious."

"Yes," said Paul. "Is this asparagus in the sauce?"

I felt like telling him it was cigarette ash.

"What about the children?" I asked. It seemed the only safe question.

"Oh, Sally will keep the children. They're better with her. But I'll see them from time to time."

"But doesn't it seem a waste," I said. I was alarmed by their calm and public dismissal of their marriage but perhaps it only seemed calm because it *was* public.

"I mean, you've been married for years and you've got the children and everything." I waved my fork in the air and Andrew took it from me and put it safely back on the table.

"I wasn't going to put it in your eye," I said crossly.

"Well, I'd rather make sure of that," Andrew replied soothingly.

"You mean," said Sally, "that we might waste our investment."

"Marriage isn't sacred," said Paul.

"Well, maybe not," I lied. "But if you make a mess of one marriage you're pretty sure to make a mess of another marriage. I mean, most couples can get on if they try hard enough. It's the effort that matters." I picked up my fork again.

"Yes, I agree," said Sally. "But Paul doesn't make the effort. He won't leave this girl."

"And is marriage worth the work?" asked Paul.

"Not if you don't work at it," I retorted neatly but I didn't feel very sure of my ground. Years of straining and pulling at each other didn't seem to have helped Andrew and myself. And I hadn't changed. I hadn't really changed at all. Andrew's face was wrinkled with disapproval and I wanted another glass of wine.

"Do you really think it's worth it?" I asked Andrew when they had gone.

"What's worth what?" said Andrew. He knew perfectly

well.

"That marriage is worth the work. I mean, we are closer than we used to be, don't you think?"

"I certainly thought so when you came back from your holiday," he said sitting back in his armchair. "But you really blew it at lunch. If you wanted Paul to fancy you you shouldn't have drunk so much."

"He drank enough himself at lunch."

"I know," said Andrew, "but somehow that's different. He's a man, after all."

# A Just Desert

SHE WISHED the dreadful nausea would stop. She was seized by another pang of sickness. God knows she hadn't anything to be sick with except loneliness and shame. The ersatz tinned meals of the day had long ago been emptied from her aching stomach and she hadn't any money to buy Vim or Harpic or a single commercial magic to dispel the sour smell of her misery. The children would be home soon and she'd have to cook them something. Well, she'd have to heat the last tin. She had no money. Soon would have no food. She had no husband and nothing to do. Only these cold quiet shining rooms. This modern masterpiece and she didn't know how to sell it, or if she *could* sell it, or who to go to for money, or whether she was legally entitled to money. She'd never been without money before. Her parents and then her husband had had enough money. Enough money for money not to be a factor in any decision. It was curious how much money mattered when you didn't have any. She was used to doing without food. She had dieted for years off and on, but now she felt ravenously hungry for solid real food. Rare steaks and fresh tomatoes. Tins of beans were all she'd been able to afford recently and now she couldn't even afford those. She'd have to go to her parents and admit it now. Admit that she'd been left, deserted. Admit that she was a deserted wife. She could hardly bear to think the words, let alone say them to her parents who would respond, she knew, with pity and curiosity. Once she'd told them she'd be jammed in the role for life. A deserted wife. Even if he came back, her parents would always think of her like that, with pity and curiosity, because she'd been left for another woman. Remembering the other woman she retched again.

At first she'd been relieved when she realised he was having an affair. It seemed somehow to justify her own coldness to him. It seemed to debase his sexuality that he had betrayed his indifferent wife. They'd been married for fifteen years and they had three children. Children of the happier passionate years at the beginning. She couldn't really remember or understand why she'd gone off sex. It had just happened somehow that days had become weeks and weeks, years. Sex was just something she didn't want to give him. She'd cook for him, clean for him, wash for him, and she did all these things with graceful resentment. She had grown to enjoy resenting him. But you couldn't combine enjoyment and resentment, or at least *she* couldn't. She knew that if she slept with him she'd stop resenting him and the resentment had become precious to her. She wasn't happy with it. She was frustrated and miserable. She just couldn't let it go. When she was a child she'd been given a doll that she'd coveted. It was entrancing. Golden curls and bright blue eyes that opened and shut as you rocked the doll. She'd taken a scissors from her mother's sewing box and hacked each golden curl from the doll's head and then, crying with rage, she'd beaten the doll's bald crown against the floor. She never knew why she had done this but she knew that she had wanted to hurt herself. Her husband wasn't like that. Deprived of warmth he'd turned towards another, brighter fire. Janine remembered the glinting fall of Miriam's red hair. That was when she'd begun to mind, when she saw that hair.

On one of the rare evenings that John had come home early she'd thought of going to see Miriam. It was a warm summer evening. John was sitting in front of the empty grate with a beer tankard and an evening newspaper. The children were shouting to each other in the garden. She suddenly felt weighted, burdened by a load of warm, unaccustomed love. As if she'd been melted by the long hot day, released and relaxed from her self-imposed misery. She went over and stood behind him. She stroked his dark wavy hair. He shook his head free of her hand.

"I'm reading the paper."

"I can see that." His rejection infuriated her. She was used to doing the rejecting.

"I'm going out." She said it to show she could leave him. "You'll have to mind the children. I've been cooped up all day and I'm fed up with them. You don't know what it's like, coping with them all day. Sticky hands and greedy little mouths. They've been asking really insane questions all day. They seem to have spasms of it, when one of them asks a question they all start."

John rustled the paper and sighed. "All right, all right, I'll look after them."

She went up to her bedroom and brushed her hair. She looked at her face with distrust. It wouldn't be hard to be prettier. Her face was thin. Her hair was greying. She looked tired and white and grubby but no amount of washing and fussing would remove that ill look. She looked as if she had just had a rather squalid sickness. Not delicate, just used. Dusty somehow. She threw the brush down. She was intelligent though. She remembered the joy she'd had when she was doing exams. Sitting up all night with cups of black coffee feeling her mind stretch away from herself and the dreariness of failing at the other, the sexual competition. Janine put on her coat and walked quickly out of the house. She left the garden by the side gate to avoid the children. She couldn't bear to talk to them now. She felt embarrassed at the thought. There was something improper about it. She couldn't talk to her children when she was on her way to peer at her husband's mistress.

The concert was being given in the National Gallery in Merrion Square and it was free. Just as well, thought Janine, I didn't even bring my handbag. She tried to avoid admitting to herself where she was going. She hadn't wanted to linger over her preparations. The Square was quiet. It always surprised her, being in the city at night. It was strange to see the wide empty streets. Few cars, no hurrying people. As if the pace of the past resumed in the evening in the graceful Georgian square.

The concert was about to begin when she arrived. The performers were squeaking their instruments in authoritative preparation. Janine felt irritated. Why can't they get their bloody instruments in order before they come here at all, she thought, as she fumbled for her cigarettes. Then she remembered that she wasn't meant to smoke and stopped. She looked up. It was a chamber orchestra and there was only one person it could possible be. A drift of stiff red hair bent over a cello. Well, she was certainly slim enough. It was a lovely figure. She was surprised at how relieved she felt. After all, what had she expected but loveliness? The concert proceeded. She hardly noticed the music at all. She wasn't musical. She'd always hated the sawing movement of the cello. She thought it obscene. She understood painting though. She'd known John was good when she met him.

"Here they are," he'd said that first day in his room. Janine had been attracted by him at once. She'd wanted to like his work because she liked him but she'd dreaded seeing it. She couldn't bear dishonesty and she'd been afraid that she'd have to stop liking him if he painted careless brightly coloured splotches. She distrusted colour in modern painting and she loved care and order.

"Oh it's lovely!" His drawing was pen and ink. Black and white. Lacy intricate patterns on ivory paper. The black was so delicately used that it seemed almost grey in places. "Oh it's really lovely." She was delighted and he'd kissed her delighted face. He felt she must really know him, to love the drawing so much.

The music stopped. Janine blinked. It was the interval. Perhaps she should go.

"Janine, what are you doing here? How's John? Haven't seen him for ages."

'He's O.K. He's lecturing. He's not drawing much though." No, he'd stopped when her love dried up. He'd become more and more involved in his job at the College of Art.

"Come and have a drink. We're giving this lot a drink afterwards, though if you'd rather wait. . . He was an assistant in the Gallery. Janine never quite knew what he did. Something to do with restoring pictures, she thought. She disliked him. His fleshy red face and his light fashionable suits. He always looked as if his arms were being dragged out of their sockets by those grudging velvet sleeves.

"I'll wait," she said. "I'd like to have a drink afterwards." Well, at least she'd really see Miriam. She needn't imagine her much longer. Would Miriam know why she was here? Would Miriam know she knew? She'd certainly tell John and then John would know because he also knew that she didn't enjoy music and that she hated the cello. Well, she couldn't go on like this. Something had to happen. She couldn't go on being insulted by her own private knowledge. As if it were her guilty secret that she knew. The music scraped and squeaked around her. The chair was hard and narrow. Perilous in fact. She felt as if she were growing fatter by the moment. Overflowing, oozing over its sides. Then clapping cracked through the high wide room. She got up, relieved that it was over.

"Here you are again, dear. Come on, I'll take you to the booze." Then, curiously, "But what *are* you doing here? I thought you loathed music." He grasped her arm and pulled her through the crowd.

"I was tired and I was walking by," said Janine crossly. "I really just wanted an excuse to sit down and look at the paintings."

"Goodness, how frank, how rude, you *are* honest." He patted her arm. Janine felt like yawning. He didn't like her. She knew that. She wondered if he knew why she was here. It was just the sort of thing he would know. He was a bit like a corkscrew. Twisted, cold and sharp.

"Here we are. Here we are. Here are our brave performers. Janine, this is Miriam." So he did know.

"Hello."

"Hello." But she was plain, really plain. Large teeth, a short nose, sandy eyebrows and eyelashes, you'd think she'd darken them.

"What'll you have to drink, Janine?" He was still holding her arm. She shook it off. She was trembling.

"I won't, I'm sorry, I just don't feel well all of a sudden, sorry, oh I'm sorry," She stumbled out of the room.

She never knew how she got home. The whole expedition had been unlikely enough. Like something in a book and, like something in a book, you assumed transport and transport happened. A taxi, she knew, but she couldn't remember how she'd managed to get one. How she'd managed to do something so efficient and heroine like. The journey was horrible. She desperately needed to get home and the taxi driver kept talking to her, reminding her that she wasn't safe at home. In her own house with her children and her husband.

"And whatever they say, it shouldn't be allowed. If it were one of my young ones I'd give him a good thrashing."

She wondered confusedly what triumph of vindictive morality he was sprouting. Why did taxi drivers always swamp her with streams of illiberal invective? Like to like, she supposed. They approved of her all right. A nice woman. A nice middle class woman nicely drying her husband out of the desert of their bed. She realised just before the taxi stopped that she had no money.

"Can you wait? I've no money, my husband has. I'll be quick. Oh I'm sorry."

The taxi driver turned around. "There now," he said. His voice was quickly soothing. "Not to upset yourself. I'll wait." Perhaps he'd begun to notice that she wasn't behaving like a nice woman at all, dashing around in taxis with no money. Distinctly not nice.

She ran towards the house. She had her key at least. John

was on his own. The children must have gone up to play records in their room. She could hear a faint rhythmic throb from upstairs. John was still reading, a book this time, in front of the grate.

"John, John, I've no money and I took a taxi from the Gallery. Oh please pay him. I can't."

"Oh God," he said. He looked at her white face and her shaking body. So she knew. He'd suspected it. It wasn't like her to want fresh air at any time, certainly not in the evening.

"O.K. I'll pay him."

She sat down but when she heard him outside she went to the cupboard and poured herself a large sherry. She didn't like the taste of any alcohol but sherry was bearable and she needed the quietening shock. She gulped it. She felt his hand on her head.

"That's where you were."

"Yes, why didn't you tell me?" The sherry went the wrong way. She coughed and coughed. He slapped her back.

"You knew anyway, what was the point?"

"No, not that." She couldn't blame the infidelity. The taxi driver had warned her about that. "Just that she's ugly. It's not even about sex, is it. It couldn't be. I mean, even I'm prettier than that. Oh God, you bastard!" She thumped him on the shoulder. "I bet you've shown her your drawings."

"It *is* about sex and I haven't." He went to the cupboard and poured himself a drink. He did this slowly. Gin, then tonic. He even opened a jar of lemon slices, extracted one, and added it to the mixture. He sipped it.

"There," he said. "Sex isn't beauty, you know. I don't care about faces. She has a lovely body and she gives it to me. She's warm. She doesn't care about my drawings any more than you care about music. She wouldn't understand them, or I don't think she would. She likes talking to me, not at me. She likes sleeping with me. She takes me as I am. She doesn't read any significance into me. She won't stop sleeping with me because I can't draw anymore."

"I didn't. You stopped drawing because I stopped sleeping with you."

"That's not what it felt like."

"I don't care what it felt like. I love you. I love the drawings too but I love you first." She put down her sherry glass. It was sticky and empty. She poured herself another.

"I don't know why I can't sleep with you. I'll try harder. I will."

The sherry, the strangely unreal evening, the emotion meeting emotion face to face after so many years, had excited her. She could. She *could* bury resentment. Throw it out.

"Janine, I don't know how to say this." He sipped his drink. "I'm sorry but I don't want you to try. It's over. I don't want you. Not any more. Not because you're not pretty or anything like that. Look, I'd have lived here and slept with Miriam if you'd let me. I'd like to live with her but I'd have stayed with you if it were possible. It's been possible. At least we could both pretend that you didn't know. I dislike my life here. Christ, can't you see what it's like for me drying up here in a a desert of your self-pity, your self-hatred."

That was odd. She'd thought of deserts too.

"I won't do it though. You'll never forgive either of us if I do. I can't live with you when you know I want to be somewhere else. You've done well with very little material. You've managed to resent me with very little cause. I hate to think what you'll do with real cause."

Janine finished her remaining sherry.

"I wouldn't, you know." She said it quietly. "I'd be much better about something that really was happening. In a way I think I'd feel better. I wouldn't have to work so hard at hating myself if something real was happening to me." She put down her glass and looked at him. He was touched by her quiet voice and sad self-knowledge. She was pleading with him.

"I can't, I can't." He shouted it. He could see his cherished flame of feeling dampened in her tears and sherry. Years of close cold knowledge, mutual knowledge, self-knowledge, unfolding like limp cabbage leaves.

"No, I hate this. I'll have to leave you. We couldn't live like that. It would be terrible. God, we both know too much. I can't do it."

He flung his glass down and went out, slamming the door. She'd taught him about resentment all right. The more you hurt, the more you have to hate.

He'd left her that night. No note, no arrangements, no money. No effort to make his actions palatable even to himself. He'd behaved disgracefully and that alone should safeguard him. He'd have to hate her for ever to make up for the empty house, the unpaid bills and the questioning children.

The nausea had passed. She wiped her cold damp forehead. A least she wasn't pregnant. That wasn't why she was sick. At this improbable thought she began to laugh and peals of hysteria echoed around the empty house.

# Some Rain Must Fall

IT WAS a calm evening. He walked home from the University in a state of self-conscious pleasure. Pleased that he knew enough to notice the daffodils against the stone walls, the gleam of slate roofs after rain. The clear watercolour air. He'd always liked Sheffield because it wasn't obvious. No lush easy beauty here. You had to work at it and discover it for yourself and Gerald liked discovering things for himself. It was one of the reasons he was such a good teacher. He distrusted the obvious and deplored students who assumed anything without working it out for themselves. He'd had a very satisfactory tutorial with a student today. The student had been misguided enough to claim that *Wuthering Heights* or the dilemma of *Wuthering Heights* was "largely unresolved". By the time Gerald had finished, the student had been almost persuaded, not quite, to read the book with special reference to the word "large". The daffodils had come out, yellow against grey in the cool slanting rain. As he approached the block of flats where he lived with his wife he noticed a smug little group of upright, pristine daffodils that had survived the winds which tossed about Sheffield's many hills. They looked so pleased with themselves there in their sheltered corner, keeping themselves nice, that he picked three. It was the sort of present that Margaret would really like. Unexpected and denoting real effort. He was always afraid that he was going to be arrested on the spot if he as much as walked on the "Don't Walk" grass, never mind raiding the Municipal flower beds. Margaret, on the other hand, was possessed of a middle class conviction that pillaging the state was positively virtuous. She could never understand that she was a different sort of middle class from his lot. "But darling, you *are* middle class," she'd say. And he'd say, "Yes, tinned salmon sandwiches on Sunday middle class, *you* have plates of the smoked stuff for parties, probably described in the tax return as business entertainment. Our lot don't *have* tax returns, we just pay tax." But she never really understood what he meant; and why should she, with a capital sum invested bringing in £3,000 a year, a present from Daddy that he hadn't at all wanted to refuse. Or wanted Margaret to refuse. It was probably giving the tax officials a headache anyway and they'd had it very easy with Gerald and his totally traceable income for years. Ripping him off to finance all those retraining schemes which, if Margaret's father could be believed, didn't happen at all. They were just good for tax. Which meant not paying it.

"My workers don't *want* to be retrained, you know." The old bastard had had a frank man-to-man chat on the subject when he was trying to justify, and, let's face it, show off his world to Gerald. "They want to keep their jobs. So I keep their jobs for them and they swear blind they've been in training with someone else in the works and somehow we keep the country going."

On one occasion old Lundy had tried to persuade Gerald to collect his old restaurant bills and give them to him. Apparently restaurant bills are tax deductible. Daddy explained that he only wanted the bills Gerald had paid when he was taking out Margaret. Since Daddy hadn't offered to pay for these meals, Gerald had refused. But old Lundy had only liked his spirit and not resented, at all, the loss on his tax returns. Gerald had been horrified. He'd gone around for weeks muttering about a new form of prostitution until he realised that he resented, above all, the fact that old Lundy hadn't offered to foot the restaurant bills. Margaret liked to eat out and she approved of going Dutch. But Gerald didn't. He liked, at least, to look as if he were paying and now here he was paying with stolen daffodils. Which Margaret would like; which was the main point.

Margaret was delighted. She'd hoped that he wouldn't mind too much about the baby and recently she'd been disappointed. He'd liked the idea very much at first. He'd made her promise ten times a day that she wouldn't let her father settle anything on the poor child but in the last few weeks Gerald had started to complain about everything to do with it.

"Cots and baby clothes are outrageously expensive, you know, Margaret. They've a captive market, you see," he'd say, putting his arms stiffly in front of him and managing to look like a willing enough captive himself. Then he'd taken to reading about the thousand and one things that could go wrong with a child's tender psyche.

"We're bound to do *something* wrong if it's intelligent but," he added morosely, "most likely it won't be." Margaret knew that the child would be everything she wanted it to be. She knew that it *would* be intelligent and for that very reason she was calm about the possibility of its being stupid. She said stupid and Gerald, who didn't want to name his dearest fear, called it not being intelligent. She knew that intelligence was vital for Gerald. It was the only tool he'd had to break out of the infuriatingly petty certainties of his parents' home.

Margaret remembered her own horror the first time she'd visited his mother. She'd known in advance that her father's wealth would be a disadvantage – Gerald had warned her about that.

"They don't like rich people," he'd announced, as if this was some rare and difficult talent of theirs.

"Well, in that case," snapped Margaret, "I won't offer them any money." But she'd been careful to dress in something nondescript. She'd ransacked her wardrobe for something that was neither too long nor too short nor too old—that might seem contrived—nor too new—that might seem too rich. Not that Mrs. Meadows would have used the word "rich". She would have said "well off" or "very you know". "You know" meant anything that Mrs. Meadows didn't approve of and "you know" was always accompanied by some graphic gesture like the rattling of imaginary coins (wealth) or the fluttering of eyelashes (anything from flirtation to prostitution—not that Mrs. Meadows saw much difference between them). Margaret had decided in the end to wear a grey trouser suit. It was good (respectable) and it was not new but it had worn well as grey flannel does. Margaret couldn't bear it because it had such sterling qualities, and that finally convinced her that it would be the very thing to warm the heart of Mrs. Meadows.

Mrs. Meadows had given Margaret one of those up and down looks that Margaret had always called impertinent. She hadn't commented on the suit or on Margaret's appearance. She hadn't needed to.

"Gerald," she said in her thin clear voice, "you know Louise, that odd girl down the road you used to go out with?"

Gerald looked embarrassed. "Can't say I remember her," he muttered.

"Of course you do," said Mrs. Meadows firmly. "Well, I saw her the other day and she was wearing trousers without even a girdle under them!"

Margaret blushed and Mrs. Meadows observed the blush.

"Oh dear," she said without sounding embarrassed at all, "how embarrassing. I didn't notice that you were wearing trousers. But of course it's quite different for you. Louise was wearing trousers to *work*."

Mrs. Meadows was quite pretty. She was plump but shapely, well corseted, Margaret thought vindictively. Her face was heavily made up and her hair was capably permed to look as if it was a wig. But why on earth does she leave those long hairs on her chin, Margaret wondered. Really, Mrs. Meadows was the kind of woman who would do it just to spite her face.

She talked incessantly and she was always busy moving things and carrying things and arranging ashtrays and plates of neatly cut sandwiches. Margaret was treated as company. She'd never really believed that people had parlours or "best" rooms. Mrs. Meadows' parlour was a real gem. There were antimacassars, pelmets, chintz and china dogs. They ate tea from plates balanced on their knees with paper napkins at the ready against the unthinkable disaster of anything spilling. Margaret hadn't even felt guilty about despising it all. It wasn't even funny. It wasn't done to please the guest. It was done to catch you out in the face of a series of hazards.

"How on earth did you manage to have tea without ruffling the antimacassars or slopping the saucer?" Margaret asked Gerald as they were getting into Margaret's car afterwards. Gerald couldn't wash up without breaking a plate or a glass, if not both.

"I didn't," said Gerald as he sat back in the driving seat. "Anyway, we usually had tea in the kitchen and we did our homework there. We did everything there. She doesn't like the idea of me marrying you so she's putting the idea away from her and the parlour's the best place for that. I bet she doesn't approve of me driving your car either. Nearest thing to admitting that I'm sleeping with you. You know," he smiled at her and pulled a bit of her hair, "my limbs resting where yours have. There's something very intimate about a car. And this is a sports car, which makes it even worse. All that power." And he revved the engine and waved to his mother who was lurking behind a curtain upstairs.

Margaret had decided, after that meeting, that there was no point in trying to placate Mrs. Meadows. Thereafter she wore her shortest or longest skirts and left dried egg on her blouse if it happened to be there. So she was sloppy but it was better than being unkind. And Mrs. Meadows *had* been unkind to Gerald. Never cruel or angry or anything you could howl about to your friends if you were a young boy growing up in North London. Mrs. Meadows had

simply used every tenet of respectability to stop Gerald
doing anything he might enjoy. His stamp collection was
"dirty", eating ice cream in the street wasn't nice and his
friends made too much noise if he brought them home
with him. But he wasn't allowed to their houses either.
"People will think you don't have a home to go to."
Well, poor Gerald. He certainly didn't have much of a
home to go to or stay in for that matter. Margaret had
loved Gerald when he had told her about his childhood.
She loved him for knowing how wrong it all was. He did
know but he couldn't escape it, though Margaret had
thought that knowing it was awful  meant that he had
escaped it. Not at all. Gerald was embarrassed where his
mother had been disapproving. He was embarrassed by
egg on blouses, unmade beds in the middle of the day and
facial hair removing cream. He even thought that
Margaret shouldn't go out to parties so much now that she
was pregnant and showing it. He hadn't said so but he'd
refused three parties recently on fairly spurious excuses. It
reminded Margaret of the time he'd refused to go into the
chemist with her.

"But why, Gerald?" she'd asked. "It's pouring rain
outside. We can shelter while I'm having the prescription
filled."

"No, it's stuffy in there. Besides I like rain," he said,
shuffling uncomfortably in the downpour.

"You hate rain. You always shelter even if you're in a
hurry. What *is* wrong?"

"Oh well. Really Margaret, any other woman would
know. I can't go in there while you're collecting the Pill,"
and Margaret had giggled until she saw that he didn't
think it at all funny.

"Come in the next time," she said. She felt that if he
pretended not to be embarrassed he'd stop *being*
embarrassed.

"I can't," he said and he looked so green and sick at the
prospect that all Margaret's tenderness for him and rage at
Mrs. Meadows had surged up and prevented her from

insisting. It had become one of the things she didn't insist on, like making the bed occasionally and washing his own socks. She didn't want to seem like a bossy wife, not after Mrs. Meadows, who was bossy in a different way. Mrs. Meadows had never bossed Gerald into doing the housework. Housework was a woman's work, and she didn't like men under her feet. So Gerald had been brought up to expect women to boss him first and wait upon him afterwards and embarrass him all the time. Well, she wasn't going to let him away with it from now on. Not with the baby on the way. But maybe she wouldn't have to fight about it. He *had* brought her stolen daffodils.

"They're lovely, Gerald, really lovely," she said as she looked at their neat crepe-paper edges. She didn't like daffodils. "Was it difficult, pinching them?"

He smiled at her slowly. "For *me* to pinch them, yes. But really, I just picked them. And what have you been doing today?"

Oh dear. Margaret didn't really want to tell him. She'd wasted a lot of money on clothes that she didn't like. She'd felt very depressed after breakfast. Gerald had grumbled about his egg (underdone) and the baby (expensive) and finally he'd refused to carry a bag of washing to the launderette. He said he was late for his lecture but Margaret knew that he didn't like launderettes any more than he liked chemists. So she'd decided to spend her latest share money on clothes and lure Gerald into a good temper with her new loveliness. She wasn't a women's magazine woman but she had a lurking respect for feminine tricks. Seduction seemed easier at the moment than argument. She was too tired and too frightened to argue the whole thing out with Gerald. He'd have to accept the baby. He'd have to stop indulging his little embarrassments at her expense, but in the meanwhile a nice new envelope had arrived this morning with her dividend inside so she'd gone shopping.

It was a hideous mistake. She should have known that whenever you were really determined to buy something you could never find anything to buy. It was a cool, rainy day and Mothercare was full of overblown women shaking damp umbrellas over racks of elastic fronted trouser suits. The pinks and blues and aquamarines glistened in the raindrops under the fluorescent lighting. The clothes were safe and dull. They'd last and last. But who wanted a maternity dress to last. Even twins didn't take more than nine months.

So she'd left Mothercare and stumbled through the windy rain to an expensive little boutique which was warm and cosy. All the umbrellas were carefully placed in an umbrella stand while you strolled over the deep pile carpet to make your choice from the models draped casually over velvet sofas. There was nothing in the shop you could wear doing housework but it all looked so desirable and pretty that Margaret bought a number of elaborate caftans which made her look more enormous than usual. Their bright colours drowned her pale, tired face but the sympathetic salesgirl assured her that she'd look marvellous if she was made up. And Gerald didn't like make up. And what would he say when he discovered that the money he'd marked off for the child had been wasted on clothes.

"I'm afraid I bought clothes, Gerald." It was a mistake to be apologetic with Gerald. He always assumed that he was in the right and made the most of it.

"*More* clothes for the baby?" Gerald shook a handful of peanuts into his hand from the bowl she'd arranged on the table. He always said he preferred peanuts out of a packet but they did look nicer in a bowl. "I should have thought the baby had enough clothes. Besides, my mother's knitting away." Mrs. Meadows plied Margaret with the kind of clothes guaranteed to make a mother's life a hell. Matinee jackets with satin ribbons which, Mrs. Meadows maintained, should always be removed before washing. "If you still use that launderette."

"No, Gerald. I know the baby has plenty of clothes, but *I* don't. I'm growing out of everything and I felt depressed this morning because you were in such a temper so I went out shopping. I felt I needed a treat."

"A treat? Margaret, I thought you realised that we needed all the money we have, and more, for the baby. We'll have to get a house soon with a garden for it to play in. And Comprehensive education's all very well but we may have to pay to educate it properly. People keep telling me that things have got worse since they abandoned the grammar schools. Won't you ever see that we can't just afford treats because you feel you want them?"

She never would see, of course. To her it was still Daddy Lundy's world where wanting to have something was a good enough reason for getting it.

Margaret had started to make the supper. She was scrubbing potatoes with great vigour and little grey scrapings whirled around the stainless steel sink.

"Gerald, we have enough money. There isn't going to be a rainy day. You have a good salary, I have a generous income, and we live on about half of all that. The baby isn't going to cost as much as two adults."

"Oh yes it is if it inherits your tastes," muttered Gerald, though he knew it was unfair. She'd tried not to be extravagant, often, though meals out and new clothes hardly counted as extravagances with her. But she was a careful housekeeper and she'd painted the flat herself. But she always said that you couldn't have an evening out at home and that there was no real pleasure in clothes that you made yourself.

Margaret had stopped peeling the potatoes. She was standing over the sink and her shoulders were shaking.

"Margaret, are you laughing?"

She turned around and her face was crumpled. She looked like a cross baby, except that real tears already streaked down her contorted face.

"I'm tired of putting up with your constant carping about money." She picked up a dishcloth and rubbed her face with it. "I'm really tired of it. If you resent having married me say so, and if you don't want your own child you can leave before it's born. I assure you I can afford it

111

on my income even if you can't afford it on two incomes. I don't need to take out massive insurances against the sky falling." She put down the dishcloth and marched towards the bedroom. Then she turned around again and her face was so ugly with rage that he wanted to slap it.

"Or perhaps you want to make quite sure you've enough money to dislike both of us, me and the baby, I mean. In comfort." And she closed the bedroom door behind her with a great slam.

In comfort. If only she knew and if only he'd been able to tell her how little comfort there'd been in disliking his mother and pitying his father. He'd been a fat boy because he always ate too much and his mother had been too middle class to let him away with that. Fatness was only a sign of prosperity in the very poor. She'd put him on a diet and after that she used to follow him around the house to make sure he wasn't eating anything on the sly. She quite quickly discovered that he was in the habit of locking himself in the bathroom with bags of cream cakes. She used to yell at him through the frosted bathroom door. "You're just like him. You're just like your father! Only with him it's whisky. My whole life is spent peering through windows, pub windows, bathroom windows, because you two want to behave like pigs. Come out at once! Come out at once!" And she'd rattle the door.

His father was a quiet, polite man who drank quietly and steadily in the pub in the evening. He always drank whisky. Nearly half a bottle of it every night. Gerald never knew whether he liked the whisky or the pub or whether he just wanted to get away from his wife and her terrible need to climb into someone else's head. In the end his father's drinking had accelerated. He'd got ill and had to stay at home and apparently he needed more whisky for that.

"Gerry, get me a bottle and keep the change," and his father would hand him a fiver and Gerald never needed to be told to hide either the whisky or the money from his mother. It was a polite arrangement. Neither Gerald nor his father ever referred to the necessary secrecy and they were both careful to conduct their transactions when "She" was out of the house, so the bottle or the money could be handed over openly. His father died of cancer, not of drink, but Gerald didn't have time to clear away the bottles from under the bed after his sudden death at home. And Mrs. Meadows found them and said nothing at the time. But a couple of months afterwards he was shocked to hear her telling his sister that she should be careful whom she married.

"Your father drank himself to death and he killed himself with our money. So be careful you don't marry a man who drinks." Was it rage because he'd escaped her by drinking and then by dying or was it just another, particularly vividly illustrated warning. Gerald had been glad, then, that his father had died early because he knew that he really would have become an alcoholic if he'd had to withstand the pressure much longer.

He could still hear Margaret crying through the bedroom door but he felt that he had no comfort to offer her because he didn't really know now what the quarrel was about. He was tired of trouble and quarrels, and Margaret's tears and his mother's anger were getting mixed up in his head. Besides, he was very hungry, and clearly there was going to be no meal without a reconciliation. He made himself two large bread and butter sandwiches with doorsteps of bread but when he'd made them they looked so like the sort of disgusting food he used to eat behind the bathroom door that he decided to go out and have a sensible meal in a restaurant. Without Margaret. If she wanted to come she could come out and say so or speak to him or something and at this prospect he crept rapidly out of the flat.

Margaret heard the door click. He'd probably gone out for a meal, the greedy great pig. Without her. She would have come out and at least tried to talk all this money business over only she really didn't feel very well and if she told him so he'd probably be nice to her – he was always very gentle with her if she was ill. She didn't want to get sidetracked this time by illness or niceness. She wanted to know why he was so terrified about the baby and money, why he had to have his little insurance policies. She'd always accepted his peculiar attitude to money before because she knew she was privileged and indulged and he had never been either. But he was now. He had worked his way into privilege and it was high time he accepted it. Really, her stomach was very sore. It was probably more of that wind the doctor had been so pleased to warn her about. Gerald had worked his way up and she'd come down. She felt very hot. Or maybe she'd always been down and just never noticed it before. Her father used to call her his "little lady," which was patronising enough. But it had never felt like that because she'd had such a nice time being little and his lady. Had he loved her mother? It was difficult to know. Her mother had always been busy organising things and sitting in the Oxfam shop or on some committee or other. She was usually busy in the evening with some sensibly religious project but Margaret never missed her when she was out. When she came home from school she'd sit on the stairs with her homework and wait for her father. He'd come through the front door into the moss-like dimness and shout, "Where's my little lady?" and then he'd take her out to dinner if he was alone. When he brought friends home he'd allow her to stay up and help him cook the lobsters or drain the asparagus. It had been fun. Trivial fun perhaps. Sinister fun maybe. But why on earth not have fun? Her friends at college had told her that she was in love with her father. She knew that she wasn't. She was in love with fun and luxury and good food. And being petted. Not the tender safety of a mother's bosom for her. It had never been offered. But her father had intoxicated her with his admiration and his glamour. She'd been bought by Daddy who'd cossetted her and spoiled her and then she'd sold herself to Gerald who hadn't spoiled her at all.

She did wish that pain would stop. It was sort of

rhythmic. One, two, three.

Gerald had been entranced with her money and her sports car and her careless rich ways, which made her appear both more generous and more secure than she really was. She'd met him when she was about to graduate and by then she'd found out about Daddy's big girls and it felt as if her only security was gone. So Gerald didn't know what he was getting. Well, neither did she. She hadn't known that money made all the difference between being cossetted and being used. The trouble was that she hadn't been brought up to insist on her rights as a person. Her father had always implied that there was some kind of advantage in being a woman, in being his little girl. So she hadn't known how to teach Gerald about equality because she didn't really know what equality was.

She screamed and it was as if the scream was something that had happened to her and not something she'd done herself. It wasn't wind at all. There was something wrong and she didn't know what to do about it. How did you ring for an ambulance? They were always telling you but she couldn't remember now, and would an ordinary ambulance do for a maternity case. But perhaps it would turn out to be wind after all and they'd just think she was fussing. But she knew it wasn't wind and because she was as frightened of the hospital as she was of losing the baby she picked up the phone and rang her father's office. When she knew he was on his way with efficiency and help she felt safer immediately and it occurred to her that it was a good thing Gerald *wasn't* there, her father would be much more use and she would never have dared phone him if Gerald had been there.

Gerald felt much better after dinner. It was strange how normal activities like eating or sleeping restored your sense of proportion. He should have brought Margaret with him but he could go home now and be nice to her on a full stomach. When he got home the phone was ringing. He heard it from half way up the stairs of the apartment building and he ran up the last flights of concrete steps. He always was excited by the sound of a phone ringing, any phone ringing. He felt that the sound of a phone ringing was one of the few remaining enchantments. He used to get excited about going abroad, when people still called it abroad. When it *was* abroad. But now there was no abroad about the places that used to smell of garlic and Gitanes. They still smelt the same but the smell didn't promise anything but more modern tower blocks and the increasing availability of Fanta (you could get it in Ghana, he'd been told) and nourishing, dull, American hamburgers. But a phone was like a telegram or a letter: it promised news or, at the very worst — and it wasn't a bad worst — gossip.

The door of the flat was open and swinging on its invisible hinges in the breeze the architect of the building had designed to go with the transient people who lived in the flats, but Gerald hardly noticed the careless, open aspect of the flat before he answered the phone.

"Gerald, Lundy here. I've been trying to get you all evening. You were out," old Lundy grumbled in an indignant whine.

"Yes, I was out, didn't Margaret tell you?"

"No, she couldn't, how long have you been home anyway?"

"I've just come in."

"Oh. I see, yes. Well I'm afraid I've a bit of bad news for you." As the phone whirred quietly in his ear Gerald could almost hear Daddy Lundy's gruesome glee. "Margaret's lost the child. It would have been a boy," he added sadly and now his voice had lost its hectoring note.

"It *was* a boy," said Gerald as he sat down on the chair in front of the telephone table. He felt as if all the blood was draining out of him. He felt white in the face and flabby.

"Is Margaret all right?"

"Oh yes. I got there in time She rang me, you know. She just lost the baby."

116

Just. How much more could she lose? But that wasn't fair. Daddy Lundy was upset. It would have been a boy.

"Can I see her? Now?"

"Yes of course. She wants you and the hospital says you can come. But Gerald?" Daddy Lundy's voice was thin with strain.

"Yes?"

"If I can help in any way. I know you don't want my money at all," — a gusty sigh — "but sometimes money helps." He sounded genuinely embarrassed. He sounded as if he knew something about Margaret that Gerald himself didn't know yet.

"Helps what?"

"She's upset and she loves you. Just go to the hospital. St. Mary's round the corner, private ward. I insisted, you know, Gerald." Daddy Lundy suddenly sounded quite drunk. "You can buy privacy. There's nothing else, but you can still buy privacy," and the phone whirred again in Gerald's hand.

Margaret lay in her neat white hospital bed and felt fat. It seemed unfair that you should look blown up and baggy when the reason for it was gone. She'd told the doctor that she'd lost her child and he'd smiled reassuringly and told her that it was "Just a miscarriage." It didn't feel like that at all. She knew very well now why she had wanted a child so desperately. She'd wanted something to love. A baby wasn't just a thing of course, but it was so close to you and so small that loving a baby must be a bit like loving yourself. And babies always loved their mothers for a while at least. They didn't start criticising until they'd stopped being babies. She and Gerald were so overburdened with Daddy and Mrs. Meadows that sometimes she felt they couldn't see each other at all, just fractions of their parents. She was tired of it. She was tired of the sheer effort of loving Gerald, of having to tidy her spoilt childhood out of the way, of having to pity Gerald's boyhood. It might have been different if she had ever felt

117

that Gerald would let go. But he wouldn't. He clung to his resentments — his mother's meanness, his father's death — and he hoarded up money as if money could buy him back his childhood. Well, she'd had enough. She didn't want to have to turn around and try to make Gerald's world right for him ever again. In fact, at the moment she hated Gerald because he would expect her to be upset and then he would expect her to get over her upset when it suited him. Anything else would be neurotic. Well, she wasn't going to get over it because there really didn't seem to be anything to get over it for.

She was dozing off in a haze of confused resentment and pethidene when she heard his voice.

"Oh Margaret, I'm sorry. You must have had an awful time."

"Yes, I did," she said firmly. "I had an awful time but Daddy was very good, he knew what to do."

"I know," said Gerald sadly. "He told me and I know I should have been there myself. I've behaved very badly." He sounded irritated about it and he *was* irritated. He hadn't really behaved all that badly. Margaret hadn't lost the baby because of that quarrel. She'd lost it after the quarrel. There was no reason for him to feel guilty about it but he did feel guilty and this irritated him.

"Well," said Margaret in reply to the irritation in his voice, "it was cheap anyway. Daddy will pay for the hospital and we won't have a baby to support."

Gerald wasn't very impressed by her bitterness at the time. She was upset because she'd lost the baby of course, and she was angry because he hadn't been there but she'd get over that and they'd have another baby. It was all very natural and normal and medical.

Since it was "Just a miscarriage" and Margaret had been "only" four months pregnant the hospital let her out within a week. She was warned that she would be depressed and weak for some time but since this was normal it was nothing to worry about. Margaret didn't feel depressed at all. Depressed was quiet and sad and miserable, and she was raging with grief and anger though no one had really noticed this yet because she'd felt both too confused and too angry to speak much to anyone while she was in hospital. When Gerald had come to sit with her in the evenings she'd pretended to be too tired to talk to him and he had seemed to accept this. She dreaded leaving the hospital because that meant getting on with her marriage and she didn't know now what the terms of her marriage were. She loved Gerald of course but she didn't really want to be alone with him at the moment. She wanted someone to look after her and fuss over her. Someone like Daddy. The flat would be in a mess and Gerald would have to be bullied into cleaning it up. Most probably she'd give in again and clean it herself.

"Come and stay with me, Maggie. For a little while anyway. Gerald can move in too. The house is enormous." Daddy had come in the night before she was to leave hospital. He had brought great sheaves of lilac which would have to be left behind for the other patients.

"Mrs. Warren will look after you," – Mrs. Warren was the housekeeper – "and your Mother's away at the moment. So it'll be like living on your own except that you'll have someone to look after you."

"You're very sweet, Daddy, but it's all right," said Margaret, not feeling at all sure that it *was* all right. "But Gerald will look after me."

"Oh well," Daddy frowned at the cellophane packages of flowers which lay at the end of the bed and Margaret thought for a moment that he was going to say that it was her funeral.

"I just offered. Make sure he *does* look after you." His heavy face folded in concern. "Don't let him disappear off into the night without a word to anyone. You didn't know where he was that night, and you were very upset. I don't know if there's anything wrong between you two and I won't ask, but he shouldn't have left you alone like that with the baby on the way."

"But Daddy, he didn't know I was going to lose the

baby."

"Yes I know, but still."

But still. Really it was a bit hard on poor Gerald. She'd been blaming him all week. Oh she'd known it wasn't his fault, but still. And she relaxed in a faint anticipation of pleasure and waited for Gerald's visit. Nothing more heart warming, really, than feeling sorry for someone, she thought sleepily.

She woke up to find Gerald's untidy head swinging above her.

"Hello, Gerald. I've been thinking and I'm so sorry that I've been so silent and difficult since I came in here. I haven't been feeling very well, you know. I suppose I'm depressed." She knew he'd accept that.

"Yes," he said. "I thought you probably were but you'll soon get over it. You look a bit better already." His face retreated so she sat up uncomfortably in the hard hospital bed. It was difficult, this sitting up, because the bed was furnished with a strange device which propped you up if the nurse had arranged it. She couldn't manage it at all on her own. The support tended to clang backwards and forwards when she tried to wedge it while the clean hospital pillows plopped neatly down the back of the bed.

"I can't do this, can you?" But Gerald couldn't. He gazed helplessly at the swinging support panel and spread out his hands. Men ought to be able to do something, she thought. Something, anything, and what was it going to be like at home.

"I can go home tomorrow Gerald but they" – oh the authority of "they" – "think I shouldn't do too much just yet, you won't mind making your own meals will you?" It would be ghastly. He *would* mind. He'd starve himself rather than cook and he'd get headaches which would leave him too weak to do anything for her. She was sloppy by nature but whenever she was ill she liked her surroundings to smell of lavender furniture polish and fresh flowers. She liked to have clean sheets and pillows and the thought of tidy rooms in the back of her mind. Well, she'd have to put up with piles of unwashed dishes and an unmade bed. Maybe there was some point in hospitals. At least they told you not to worry. She watched Gerald's bland creamy face dreaming out of the window and muttered to herself, "Do worry. Do worry. Do worry."

"What?" She'd seemed so much better today. She'd even smiled at him. And there she was muttering away to herself.

"I said 'Don't worry'," said Margaret. "I know it'll be difficult when I go home but Daddy said that we could stay with him if you liked." Bless Daddy that he hadn't thought, at all, of what Gerald liked.

"Oh, well actually that's what I wanted to ask you about." If only they were at home, he and Margaret. Somewhere he could explain things to her without the nasty feeling that there was a nurse flickering around the corner on angel wings, waiting to catch him out.

"Margaret, Mummy rang," he said, curling his toes inside his leather boots the way he used to curl them when his mother screamed at him. Only then his toes were dirty and exposed in horrid little sandals and you could see them squirming. "Mummy rang and offered to come and look after you. When you come out of hospital. She said she knew about miscarriages, and she offered."

"I bet she knows about miscarriages, she's had enough of them, miscarriages of justice I'd call them." Then it occurred to Margaret that Gerald might have refused the offer. "No, I'm sorry Gerald, that was cruel. I didn't mean it. It's just that she's hurt you so much. What did you say?"

"Yes."

Well she'd rung him up from London (the expense!) and offered him something he wanted for the first time. He knew Margaret's depression was natural but he was hurt by her total withdrawal all the same. He'd visited her every evening and every evening she had pretended to be asleep. She'd excluded him as if she had forgotten that he, too, had some reason for distress. And Mummy had suddenly rung up and offered to make up for the neglect of a childhood when he was feeling as frightened and lonely as he'd felt as a boy. Practically speaking, Mummy solved a few problems. *He* couldn't look after Margaret when she came out of hospital. First of all she wouldn't talk to him in hospital so she'd probably want to talk a great deal once she got out of hospital about why she wouldn't talk to him when she was in hospital. Over wine and little contrived meals that he'd have to collect from the delicatessen, Mummy would look after Margaret. She must want to or she wouldn't have offered. Mummy would certainly see that the flat was tidy and clean and that Margaret got enough to eat and not too much to drink. And Mummy had done it, offered it for him, Gerald. He couldn't throw such a gift back in her face.

"Yes? You actually said yes. Are you mad? Do you not care about me at all?" Margaret sat bolt upright in the bed. Her hair stuck out around her thin pink face in greasy spikes and her appearance startled Gerald. She looked so angry and vivid and there. She didn't look at all like a pallid invalid who had to be looked after and accommodated. He wouldn't have dared hand her over to Mummy if he'd thought of her like this. The hospital had been telling him so much about her (better today, bound to be depressed, quite normal) that he'd begun to think of her as mindless and of no account in an argument, just a figment of the hospital's imagination.

"Gerald, if you let your mother look after me I'll go and stay with Daddy. He offered you know. I said no, because it seemed so weak to run to Daddy whenever something went wrong. Well, it *was* weak but at least it makes some kind of sense. He's always been kind to me, however much you may have disapproved of it. He's always been kind and your mother's never even been kind to *you*. How do you really think she'd behave towards me, or didn't you care? I suppose it doesn't matter to you how *I* feel as long as you don't have to look after me." Margaret was swaying backwards and forwards in her effort not to lean back against those embarrassing pillows.. "But it's not even as if you were worried about looking after me, is it? You wouldn't do that anyway. But you didn't want it to look as if you were neglecting me. You wanted to look like a responsible caring husband and I'll have to pay for your image of yourself. It'll be fun for me, won't it? I can have little carouses with Mummy while you're out late finishing a very important chapter. Gerald, I won't do it. If you don't tell that bitch not to come I'm going to go and stay with Daddy and you can tell your mother I've left you." She was almost crying but she knew she mustn't cry. If she cried, Gerald would comfort her and she'd end up agreeing to put up with Mrs. Meadows and they'd whirl round and round again in the same confused jumble. Mummy didn't give me a childhood, you give it to me, Margaret. Daddy looked after me Gerald, you look after me. Mummy neglected me Margaret, let her neglect you.

"Margaret, you're still weak and you're just allowing this to upset you. Mummy won't stay long and I can't refuse to let her help, can't you see that?"

"No," said Margaret, "I can't and there's the bell. Visiting time's over. You'd better go. Are you going to put her off?"

"I can't. Please Margaret, try to see my point of view."

"Oh I can see it. I never seem to see anything else *but* your points of view. Don't bother to collect me tomorrow," she said and lay down in the bed and closed her eyes. Gerald looked at her for a few minutes and decided to leave it. She'd change her mind, or at least she'd allow herself to be collected tomorrow. He kissed her rigid face and left her.

When Margaret was quite sure that he'd gone, she climbed uncomfortably out of bed and went in search of a telephone. She was afraid that one of those bossy nurses would catch her and tell her about her stitches or her depression or something but she managed to creep along the dim glossy cream corridors without running into anyone. And she found a call box. It was fortunate that she'd been listening to the radio so much lately. People

123

were always ringing up from hospitals in radio dramas, so Margaret had discovered that you didn't need any cash to phone out from a hospital. The operator knew and cared. Maybe there was some advantage in being ill. Even Daddy had forgotten to leave her any cash and it had never occurred to Gerald. The radio was right. The operator gave her a free call and Daddy answered. He was half asleep but he promised to send a car. But Margaret didn't want a car. She wanted to go home with Daddy and have it all made up to her.

"Daddy, couldn't you come too? Just to take me home?"

"I would have liked that, Maggie. I really would. But you told me you weren't coming home so I've just confirmed a very important date in Paris." He sounded quite excited. "I was going to invite her over here if you were coming home. You could chaperone us," he giggled. What *was* he talking about? "You see, I'm getting married again. Your mother wants to go her own way and I've been lonely, particularly since you left home, and you'll like Natalie. She's French," he said as if that settled it.

There wasn't much else to say except good luck and bring her to see me and Margaret managed this though she felt sick and her face was cold and damp.

"I'm very pleased, really Daddy. I hope you'll be very happy but I don't think I'll go home if you're not there. I'd prefer the flat if I could have it."

"Now Maggie, you'd be happier at home with Mrs. Warren. She'd look after you. Mind you, Gerald might prefer the flat. Less plutocratic, you know."

The flat was an executive apartment for accommodating anything from company whores to company investments and Margaret hated it but she moved in there the next day before Gerald could possibly turn up at the hospital to collect her.

It was empty and clean and so dismally well designed that it could never be untidy. You couldn't clean it up. There was nothing you could do with it but crawl into bed and hope to find yourself an interesting job soon. And she didn't need to do that. Not with £3,000 a year. She did go to bed.

She was cold though the flat was warm in a dry unsatisfying way. She longed for the sympathetic heat of a coal fire and despised herself for it. "I must be getting like something in an ad. A National Coal Board ad," she said to herself as she was going to sleep and at that she woke up with appalling suddenness. She *was* going mad, that's how it began, you talked to yourself, and she'd felt pretty mad all day. She hadn't understood a single thing she'd done today. It had all seemed the right thing at the time. Leaving Gerald had seemed as inevitable as running away from a tiger in a dream. She used to have dreams like that. She'd run and run, up the walls and over the ceilings, and finally the tiger would swallow her but it wouldn't stop there. She never woke up at that point. The tiger would swallow her but leave her alive and she'd watch the red glow of his inside which looked a bit like the intestines of a rabbit she'd once seen spilled out on the road. She was mad and she was alone and it seemed to her that if she didn't do anything about it quickly she'd be finished. Some sad official would come in a couple of days and meet her unrecognising stare. She'd be there at the end of the bed, sitting in a stiff terrified huddle. Oh really. She'd read that in a magazine.

Gerald was sitting at home in the flat and his mother was bustling about in the kitchen talking to herself in a thin, clear whisper.

"I can't understand it. Now why did she put the saucepans there? She should have had Gerald fix hooks for them on the wall. Much more economical. Of course if you have money," – deep sigh and loud cluckings. Gerald sometimes wondered if she knew how mad she sounded. She'd been very pleased about Margaret's desertion. She hadn't said so, of course. She'd nodded sensibly and said that miscarriages were like that and of course if you had money, well, you could have those kind of moods. She'd had a miscarriage herself and she'd felt a bit funny (you must have looked it too, thought Gerald viciously) but she'd had to pull herself together because after all there were the other children and not very much money.

"There were the other children," Gerald said. "You did have them."

"Yes," said Mrs. Meadows with a sigh. "They were a great burden."

A burden. Margaret would have never made a child feel itself a burden. A weight, a dampener of joy. Nothing had ever dampened his mother's joy, mind you. She never had any in the first place. She was joyless from the day she was born. Her burdens were her only pleasure.

He hadn't a clue where Margaret had gone. He'd rung her father but there'd been no answer so she couldn't be there because the doctor had said that she wasn't to go out for two weeks after she came out of hospital. Gerald had wondered about that. It seemed a little too careful, so he'd asked the doctor, who said, "It's not normal, no," and he looked at Gerald as if he were puzzled. "But she does get a bit over-excited you know."

She didn't—...less her. When he saw his mother taking up her shoddy little burden, he longed for Margaret and her excited attitude to life. She was like a child except that a child doesn't live *for* anything. It just gets excited by the day it lives in. Margaret drained her days of all their possibilities because, for some reason he'd never understood, she was terrified. She went out to dinner with a desperate bravado and she put on her make up beforehand as if she were an officer putting on his full dress uniform to go to the Duchess of Richmond's ball before Waterloo.

"*Two* pints of cream, really, of course it may have been cravings but you'd think. . . ."

Gerald never did hear what Mrs. Meadows thought because the phone rang then.

"Gerald? It's me."

"Who?" because he couldn't really believe it. He'd

never thought that what he wanted happened. He'd always believed that if he carefully and superstitiously refrained from wanting anything, he just might get it. As long as he didn't let anyone know he wanted it.

"Gerald, it's me, Margaret." She was crying, he could hear the whine in her voice. "I'm at Daddy's flat and I thing I'm going mad. And he's getting married again, oh please come. You know the whore flat. That's what you call it. I'd even put up with your mother. I don't mind. Please come."

She'd hated it when he called it the whore house. And he'd laughed and said all right, whore flat. The other side of Daddy, that's what she'd always thought, but Gerald said that Daddy was no hypocrite. He only *had* one side, God help him. But Margaret had always thought that *she* could help him instead of God. It was unreasonable. She shouldn't be angry that the old fool was getting married again. But it helped to call him an old fool. She was cold again and she felt sick but Gerald had said that he'd come immediately so she might see him before she went completely mad. It was strange but she was sure that Gerald would be less embarrassed about her being mad than Daddy. Daddy thought that "nutters" should be put out of their misery. "They're no use to themselves and they make their people suffer. I wouldn't let a dog I liked go through that." Daddy didn't like dogs.

Margaret clung to the sides of the mattress but it was a foam mattress and it bent upwards and slipped out of her grasp. She lay down. She felt safer in bed but she wished she had a hot water bottle. She'd stay in bed until Gerald came. If he did come. She'd never believed that anyone but Daddy could love her and Daddy loved her because she was his. But her Mother never had. There must be something unlovable about her if her mother looked tired at the prospect of building a sandcastle on a beach for a fat little girl. A fat little girl who made her mother's eyes droop with weariness. "We have to go home now, the sun's too hot and I've a headache." Or a cold or a twinge or a pain. Margaret had learned fairly early that her mother's pleasure was her work. She was a proud child and she didn't want that. She didn't want to be anyone's burden. It was going to be difficult being mad but perhaps she wouldn't notice.

The doorbell ding-donged in no urgent way. Apparently executive flats didn't suffer from urgency. She climbed out of bed and opened the door.

Gerald was standing there. His hair was wet and his hands were hidden behind his back.

"I've got a present for you, Maggie." He smiled at her and he looked quite drunk.

"Are you drunk?" Margaret had quite forgotten about being mad.

"Yes," he said. "I thought it might be more fun to drink behind the bathroom door but it wasn't. So I brought you a present," and he threw a "No Parking" sign on the ground. "I stole it," he said, "from the Council dump. I didn't saw it off myself but you can't have everything. I don't *approve* of it but I thought you might like it. Can I come in?"

"No," said Margaret. "You can take that thing back to the dump and then you can come back here and ring your mother and tell her you're staying the night in Daddy's whore house."

"I can't do that," said Gerald.

"No, I know you can't, but still," and she felt her face smiling.